TAINTED BONDS

A Destruction of Gods Novella

K.R. RICHARD

CONTENT & TRIGGER WARNINGS

Tainted Bonds is a Dark Fantasy Romance novella that is strictly meant for readers over the age of **18**.

It contains a wide variety of adult content that may be triggering for some readers. This is a list of those triggers, but understand that not all may have been listed.

If you find something that needs to be added to this list, do not hesitate to get in contact with me so I may add it in.

I ask that every reader takes this page seriously so that everyone's mental health is protected.

- **Sibling Rivalry**
- **Sexual Content**
- **Talk of SA**
- **Physical Abuse**
- **Mental Abuse**
- **Child Abandonment**

- **Betrayal**
- **No HEA**

If you find yourself relating to any of the characters in my book due to their trauma, just know that I see you. You are not alone, and you are worth every breath that you take.

DEDICATION

*For everyone who has told me that blood is thicker than water,
fuck you.*

Bonds can be broken. New ones can be made.

Love is handcrafted, not passed on.

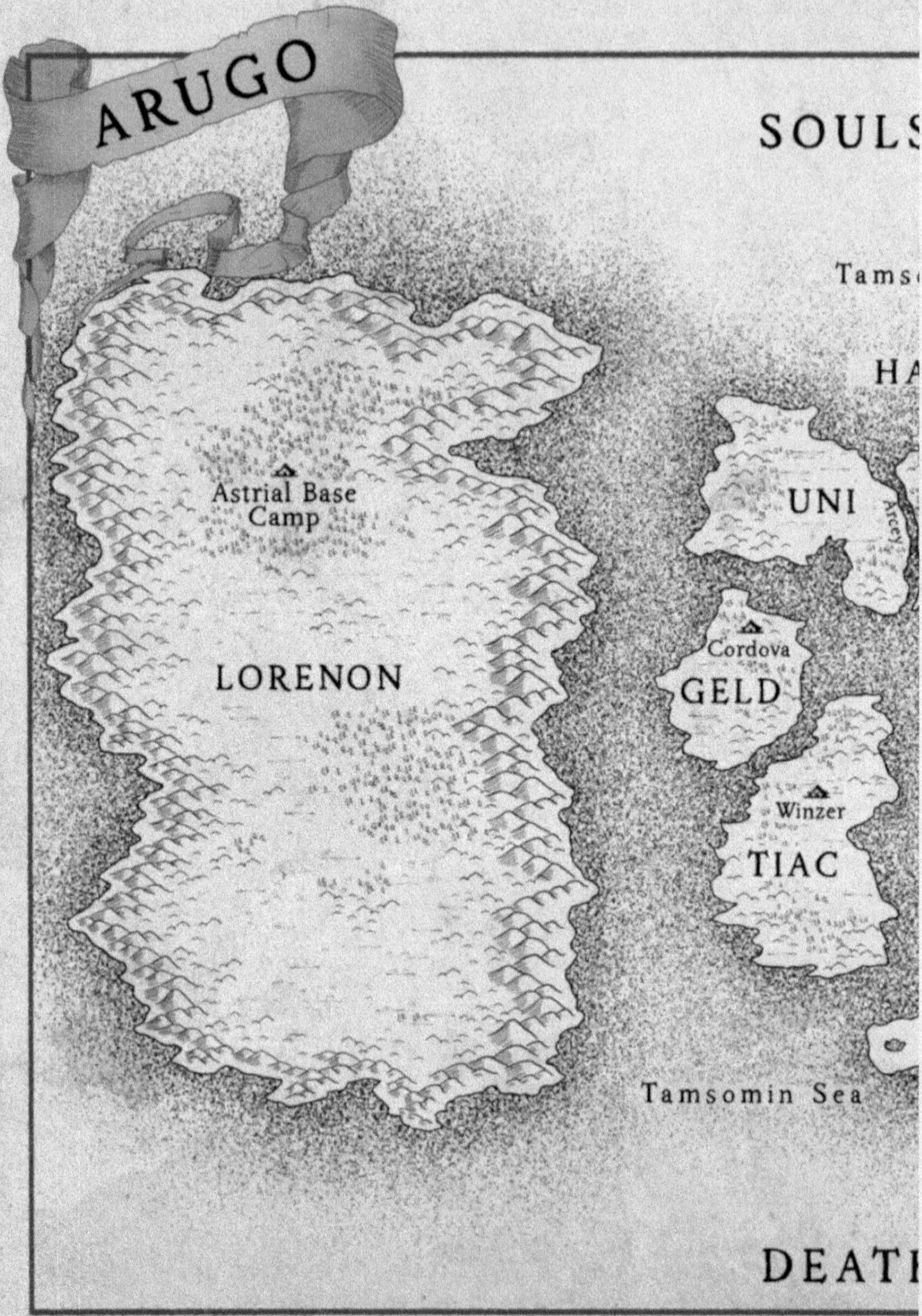

ARUGO
SOULS
Tams
HA
UNI
Arce
Astrial Base
Camp
LORENON
Cordova
GELD
Winzer
TIAC
Tamsomin Sea
DEATH

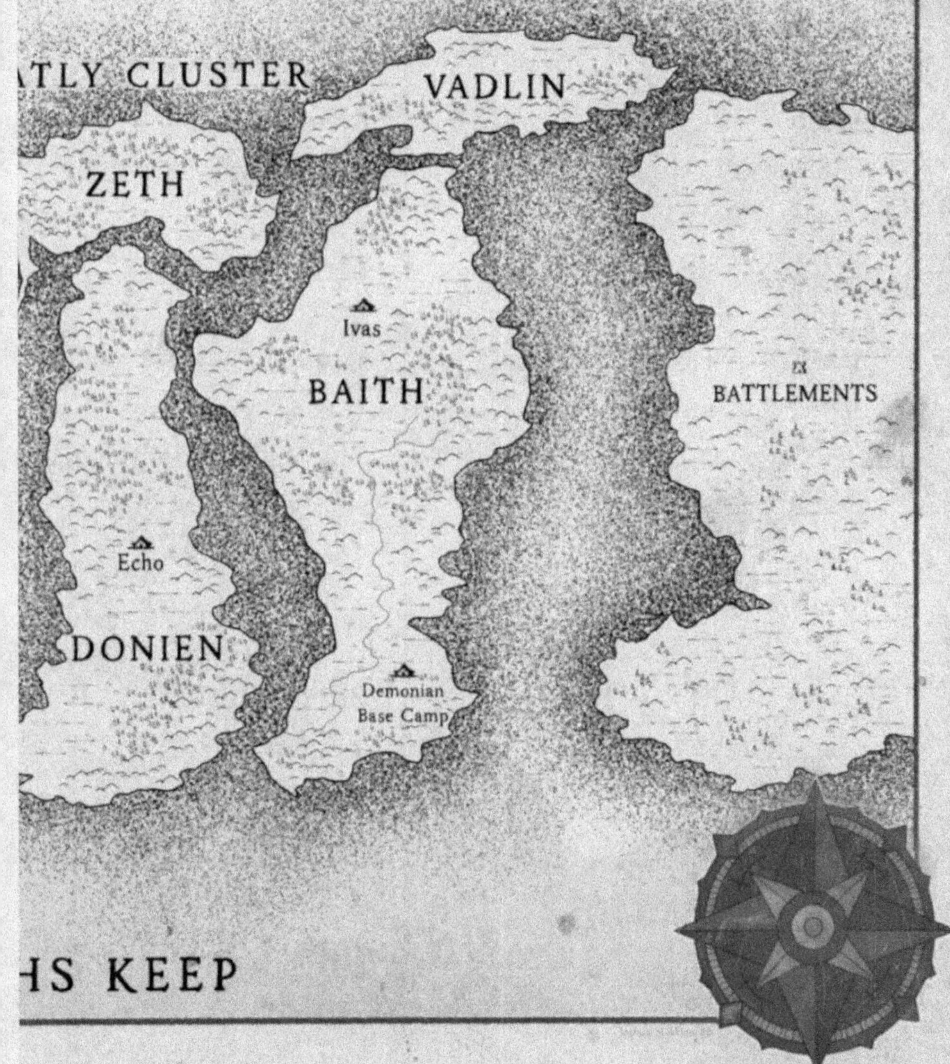
S HAVEN
omin Sea
ATLY CLUSTER
VADLIN
ZETH
Ivas
BAITH
IX
BATTLEMENTS
Echo
DONIEN
Demonian
Base Camp
HS KEEP

Pronunciation Guide

The Home of Light and Shadow

Nether - NEH-thur

Worlds

Arugo - AH-roo-go
Sytherac - SITH-uhr-ak

Places

Baith - BAYTH
Battlements - BAT-ul-ments
Donien - Don-EE-un
Geld - GELD
Lorenon - LORE-non
Orical Ocean - OR-ih-kul OH-shun
Tamsomin - tam-SO-min
Tiac- TY-ak
Uni- yoo-NEE
Zeth - ZETH

Gods

Etbris- ET-bris
Lixtis- LICKS-tis

Astrial Angels

Elena - EE-lee-nuh
Enzo - INZ-oh
Jackal - JAK-uhl
Quinnie - KWIN-ee
Soran - SORE-uhn
Vanora - vuh-NOOR-ah

Demonians

Bashtian - BASH-tee-uhn
Hinchy - HIN-chee
Mariem - mah-REE-uhm
Matryles - mah-TRA-els
Torrien - toh-REE-en
Winzer - WIN-zuhr
Zoe - ZOH-ee
Zorro - ZOR-oh

Shadow Hound

Fletcher - FLETCH-er

I

BONDS ARE MADE

1,296 A.B.

496 Years Since the Beginning of The Eternal War

I

ETBRIS

When using his ability to make the creatures around him, Etbris did not expect to grow so fond of them. In fact, it caught him off guard that his heart could feel such a vast amount of love. He thought since the day he was molded from darkness, nothing would fill the emptiness in his chest.

It was not until the very first reptilian beast cracked from his dark green egg, speckled with deep brown, that Etbris knew he stood a chance at filling the void inside of himself.

The God of Death took great care of everything he made from his own hands, just like he knew Shadow would have wanted him too. He picked the pieces of each creature with every ounce of patience that resided in his short, slim frame. He only wanted the best for them, and that meant taking the time to find the perfect ingredients to make sure everything that came from him had all it needed to be able to thrive.

Etbris only wanted them to know what it was to be happy and at peace with how he created them.

Watching each different creature grow was the highlight of his life and the only thing that brought a true smile to his face.

Etbris can still feel the scales as they glide across his fingertips. The tufts of fur that would grace the delicate skin between his fingers, and even the slimy substances that would cling to the backs of some of his more unique creations.

The phantom feelings often draw him into his mind, back to the time when he could sit and watch all his precious things live in harmony in the world he created for them, Sytherac.

Mapping out each region of the world and tailoring it to be a sanctuary of solitude was all that he'd worried about at the time of its creation.

It was never meant to be a home for anything or anyone else.

That is, until his hate-filled brother, Lixtis, ruined everything that Etbris loved so much.

Sending his malevolent Astrial Angels and those mutts made of light to torture and maim his peace-filled creatures. The memories still make him sick to his stomach.

Each different cry for help haunts him, even in the deepest of sleeps. Etbris has never forgiven his brother, nor will he ever. The damage caused is too much to mend.

Now, as he sits behind his office table with his legs crossed under him, Etbris's anger rises to the surface of his skin. He keeps his eyes pressed closed as he works to control his breathing.

"Memories are the past, and today I will live in the present." Etbris takes another calming breath as a knock sounds on his office door.

"Come in, Bashtian." There is no second guessing who is on the other side because he has learned the rhythms of each Demonian warrior allowed to enter his personal chambers.

As the door gently swings open, the towering figure shows his pearly white teeth in a wide smile.

"Good evening, sir. I came to fill you in on the latest updates we received from the front lines." Bastian waits just on the other side of the threshold with a handful of dull white parchment. The monthly battlefield reports make Etbris sit with unease. Each scribble of black ink tells the details about his fallen warriors and the hardship that he has sent them into. Guilt always finds a way to sink its venomous fangs deeper into Etbris, so much that he does not recall a time when he was not constantly being bitten.

The only thing that he is grateful for every month when Bashtian greets the confines of his office is that the time between the reports has gradually gained more space. What started as a daily occurrence soon became weekly and now, monthly.

Etbris returns the smile, but his is not as bright as the winged man's in front of him.

"Go on then, take a seat and fill me in." Bashtian moves his upper body to the side just enough to fit his featherless wings through the doorway.

Etbris did not make his palace accommodating to beings with wings since he has such a distaste for his brother's Astrial Angels, but after the massacre of his creations on Sytherac, Etbris did what he had to do.

He made his own winged beings that have sound bodies and minds much like himself, who would fight against his brother's in a battle that seems to never end.

The Eternal War.

A war that should have never been waged to begin with, but insanity sunk its fangs into Lixtis. Now it is brother against brother. Astrial Angels against Demonians, and nothing will change that besides the downfall of one or the other.

Etbris watches as Bashtian, the first Demonian created by his hands, folds his legs across each other on the floor of his office. The God does not keep chairs in his personal chambers because he likes the feeling of being close to the ground. Etbris loves the sensation of the energy traveling through all of creation around him. Being close to the minerals in the earth gives him a better chance to connect himself with everything around him and beyond him.

The blackness of the walls and floors almost blend in with the onyx fabric of the warrior's uniform. If not for the deep black of the stones that built the palace and how they shine an unnatural shade of black, Bashtian may have disappeared against its surface altogether.

"Zoe sent over a full report of the movements of the Astrials. She said that Vanora does not seem to be moving with the new wave that Lixtis sent to Battlements."

The statement does not surprise Etbris in the least because he would never expect his brother to give up something so valuable to him like Vanora. As soon as Etbris saw the way Lixtis looked at the Astrial woman, he knew that nothing good would come from whatever relationship grew between them. It is something that the God of Death has thought about often because he genuinely feels sorry for anyone that has to live in his brother's shadow. He cannot bring himself to think about the horrors the ones that serve the God of Souls have to witness. The pain they must go through just to survive a day in the area above Arugo that is cloaked by clouds.

Bashtian pauses as he flips through the stack of parchment in his grasp. Etbris's solid black eyes watch the ease with which the other's hand moves and the way the blackness at each fingertip has spread closer to his palm than the last time he saw him. A sign that the power residing in his veins needs a release. The only safe way for that to happen is to have Bashtian far away from Death's Keep. Etbris thinks that maybe it is time to send his firstborn to the front lines of Battlements. There he can expel his shadows and only cause harm to those that deserve it.

"We lost four hundred and nine warriors in the last wave. Most were first years, but we did lose Tiac and his handler, Winzer. Zoe counted six hundred and seventy-four Angels down." Bashtian takes a moment before looking up from the pages. His dark brown eyes tell Etbris all he needs to know: Bashtian is worried. Losing anyone in battle is rough, but losing the last of the guardians is heart-shattering. Each different scaled reptilian creature was a symbol of what came before, a time when Etbris crafted freely and without worry.

Now, the God does not make anything. After making his Demonians, he gave up the art he cherished out of fear of losing even more than he already has. All of the Demonians love deeply, so none of this is easy for them. Etbris made them that way so that they never want to see another war in their lifetime if the one currently being fought ever ends.

It does not surprise Etbris that his last guardian finally met his end. The old four-legged serpent fought well over the centuries.

He will become the namesake of the last unnamed island of The Hatly Cluster, and his handler's name will be the name of any town that may develop. It is the least he can do for their hard-fought battle, and they can rest easy beside the ones gone before them.

"All of which weren't at their full wingspan, so we can suspect they are only sending over their weakest or newest warriors. Mariem added that the medical tent is running low on the supplies needed to mend the wounds from the Birth Light."

Etbris nods his head as the words seem to die in the air between them.

"You need to head to Battlements. Zoe is strong but not as strong as you, nor is she seen as such a threat. If Vanora comes in this next attack and you are not there to go sword to sword with her, then we are dead." Etbris watches the warrior's face go from relaxed to stone cold in a flash. The God knows that Bashtian will not leave him here willingly, so if he has to use their second biggest enemy as a tool, then he will.

"Bashtian, I made you to be a protector. Not just a protector of the other Demonians or any creations I may make, but even of the Astrials that my brother cares nothing about. Vanora and Lixtis would rather send children to the battlefield if it means they can enjoy the show." Etbris does not try to soften the blow of his words when he talks to Bashtian. If he did, then he would not be the God he needed to be.

"Zoe has been holding the front lines for centuries now, and I know you have been waiting for the chance to get your hands bloody. Do you want to go?"

Bashtian does not hesitate to answer, "Yes, I will go, and I will fight for every innocent life on that battlefield and off of it."

Pride grows inside of Etbris as he sees the good that has come from the Demonian warrior he created.

"If I come face to face with Vanora, I will not think twice about bringing her to her knees. The lives of thousands are on her hands and her masters'. It is time one of them answered for all that they have done." Bashtian's voice is full of certainty when he speaks, and it leaves Etbris with a renewed hope for peace.

The worry that graced Bashtian's eyes moments ago is gone, like it was never there. A fire is beginning to burn behind the warrior's gaze that sits across from Etbris, and it is that fire that sets him apart from the other Demonian's.

Where the others would let the anger consume them entirely, Bashtian lets it simmer, only placing enough fuel to keep the flame alive but not out of control. The strength to hold his rage in place is only one of the things Etbris loves about his son.

LIXTIS

The sound of skin hitting skin vibrates through the throne room. It sits right inside the giant double doors made of crystal that welcome you to the palace made of clouds, The God of Souls' home.

"How dare you question me!" Lixtis's voice booms through the open expanse of space as a red-haired Astrial woman kneels on the ground in front of him.

She sits unmoving from her spot as a white strip of fabric hangs from her face, covering her eyes. The air around the pair comes to a standstill as Lixtis raises his foot behind his back just before sending it to connect with the Angel's stomach in one smooth motion.

The woman lets out a gasp and catches herself on her palms as she falls to the ground. Lixtis reaches down with his golden brown hand before she can catch her breath, snatching the white cloth from her face, granting her the luxury of having her eyesight back. He originally placed the cloth over her eyes so that she would not be able to prepare herself for the onslaught of his attack. Not knowing when the hits were coming made each slap across her face hurt much more.

"Look at me when I am speaking to you." He bares his teeth as his words squeeze from the tight spaces in-between. Jet black hair sits in short, tight spiral curls on the top of his head, and his light brown eyes are daggers as he watches the woman at his feet.

"I did not mean to upset you, master." The woman's voice is light like the touch of a feather and as smooth as an uninterrupted river. Her cheek grows purple with a newly blossoming bruise from the hand that struck her moments ago. Bright red hair with small wisps of gold fall to the side of her face as she raises her eyes to the man in front of her.

"I do not care what you were or were not trying to do, Vanora. You are meant to sit and listen, not to speak. If I wanted a talkative whore, then I would keep Jackal by my side and not you." Lixtis needs obedience; he craves it from everyone around him. It is why when Vanora, his first creation, mentioned that the Angels being sent to Battlements were not strong enough to stand against the Demonians, he snapped.

"I am sorry I upset you, master. I meant no disrespect to you or your name." Lixtis savors the fact Vanora is so deep in his grasp. He has always made sure she will bend to his will, no matter what it may be. Molding her is his favorite activity, besides watching her kneel in front of him as her skin wears the marks he has made.

"You are damn right, you did not." He reaches down and grabs Vanora's chin in his hand. As he tightens his grip and looks into her honey eyes, he smiles.

"Vanora, I really hate hurting you." He must suppress his urge to laugh in her face, but his smile grows larger. "You just make it so easy."

Lixtis studies the face he holds in his hand as she does not move an inch. Arousal spreads through his body at the sight of Vanora's submissiveness.

"You always do look so much better when I leave you covered in bruises, do you not, *pet*?" His words can cut anyone to the bone as they leave his mouth; his eyes zero in on the mark he left on her face.

"Yes, master." Vanora's eyes are still locked with his. Her bright white wings rest lazily behind her. They remind him of the clouds that make up his home – soft, plush, and the brightest white he could create. They are as pure as the day he made them, just like the body to which they are attached.

The only touch Vanora has ever known is his own, and that is how he likes it. She is clean of all others; nothing taints the purity that he crafted her from.

With her words still in his ears, Lixtis raises the open palm of his free hand as he positions it by his head. In an instant, another ring fills the clouds with the connection of skin on skin.

This time a new bruise will build on Vanora's white freckled skin far enough up her cheek to cause the bottom of her eye to bloom purple and black.

"Since you think I am not sending capable bodies to fight my war, then you can go in their wake." Lixtis rubs his thumb over the assorted colors of her skin. "That should give you time to think about who the ruler is here, and who the obedient little bitch is."

"Yes, master. It is an honor to be sent to fight this battle for you."

Lixtis likes the way the words fall from Vanora's light pink lips, but he finds himself growing bored of her. The same cunt is only good for so long before it is time to find a replacement.

He thinks he will call upon Jackal; a male seems like a decent alternative to what Lixtis has been toying with.

Lixtis roughly pushes Vanora's head to the side by her chin still held in his hand. Those that question him don't deserve a simple release. She already wears the colors on her skin made by him. Now, Vanora will also carry an ache in her neck as a reminder. As he walks to his throne in the middle of the room, he cannot help but take in the grandness that he sits in every day.

The chair sits at the top four steps that make him peer down at the rest of the room, showing who is truly in charge of everyone else.

Vanora still kneels at the bottom of the stairs as Lixtis sits on top of the feather-filled gold cushion that makes up the seat of his throne. The plushness underneath him reminds him of how many wings had to be plucked to suit his needs when designing his royal seat. The pearl arms are shaped like a wisp of wind, making their way to the floor where they flare out to cover more circumference to stabilize the chair.

The back of the throne has the same whisp going up the sides, and in the center rests the same gold feather-filled cushion. Each one is outlined in small golden rivets.

Lixtis thinks it is a throne meant for a God of Gods. Someone worthy of great power that can surpass the ones that birthed him and his bastard little brother. If he had it his way, then he would be the only greatness in Arugo, Sytherac, and even the Nether.

Lixtis has always dreamed about taking the place of Light and Shadow, but he must get through Etbris first. It seemed like an easy task until The Eternal War was waged; now Lixtis has begun to second guess the Angels he made. Something about the Demonians taking down his Astrial Angels so easily makes him question his creation process.

Which does not sit well with him. Lixtis does not mess up.

A movement from the distance brings him out of his thoughts as his eyes readjust to his surroundings. Vanora's wings twitch ever so slightly.

His voice sounds like he has swallowed glass as the haunting thoughts of being a mess up still weigh him down. "Leave me and be on your way to Battlements as soon as possible."

Vanora stands as she dips her head in a bow with her hands tucked to her sides "Yes, master. Do I need to bring my unit?"

Lixtis watches as her eyes stay cast downward. "Bring your unit and be out of my palace by nightfall. You disgust me."

His first Astrial Angel bows again, this time deeper, before she turns on her booted heels towards the crystal doors. Lixtis notices that her normal white and gold armor is replaced with a basic white button-down blouse and tan trousers tucked into her white uniform boots.

Lixtis does not remember when he called for Vanora, but he

thinks it could have been when she was just coming from morning training.

As he watches the double doors close, Lixtis sinks into his throne as he fishes out the medium-sized crystal ball by his side.

All he can think about now is if the King that lives under the sea of the Orical Ocean in Sytherac has heard anything about the seer woman he has been looking for to strengthen his army.

3

VANORA

LEAVING LIXTIS BEHIND AND MAKING HER WAY BACK TO THE training room where she left her unit, Vanora feels nothing.

No pain.

No sadness.

Nothing.

She does not think she has ever truly felt anything besides the pleasure forced upon her which also comes with pain, but pain has become a friend. It makes her think that one day she will feel other things.

Pleasure does not even feel like the right word to use to describe her time with Lixtis, but that is what he tells her it is. So, she believes him, and he uses her. It is a cycle she has known from the very beginning.

Her unit has been dealt the same hand except they are not their masters go-to like she is; he always finds new ways to use her body. It is not something any of them talk about, and she does not see it changing anytime soon.

Walking back into the room, Vanora is greeted by the noise of weapons ricocheting against shields and the laughter of her three lifelong friends: Elena, Enzel, and Quinnie.

As her feet step into the space, everyone pauses their task and looks at her. Squaring her shoulders, her wings rise behind her back from their relaxed state.

"Do not stop just because I came in the room; besides, we have orders to head to Battlements before nightfall." She does not hesitate to make her way through the training room, but she is soon stopped by Enzel, the twin brother of Elena. His golden hair sits parted down the middle of his head as small strands stick to the side of his face from the sweat of their training. Dark blue eyes look over Vanora's bruises just before she steps around him to continue her walk to her sword and sheath at the back of the room.

"What did he want?" Quinnie's deep voice breaks the silence of the room.

"He wanted to tell me the numbers of the ones we lost on the field," Vanora pauses as she tightens the leather strap of her sheath across her back. "Six hundred and seventy-four is the number before anyone asks."

None of them make a noise when she recites the number, but she knows what they are all thinking.

Lixtis knew they would never make it against well-trained Demonians. It was a joke sending kids to fight in an adult war.

"We have orders to gather our things and report to Battlements tonight. He wants us at the front lines to eliminate any Demonians that threaten to take any more of the land under our feet." Vanora walks back across the room as the ones around her prepare themselves for travel.

"What about your face?" Quinnie asks as she catches up to Vanora's right side, her light brown hair slapping the base of her equally as light brown wings at her back.

"Yeah, what happened, Nora?" Elena places herself to the left of Vanora asking the question in an almost silent whisper. She has never been one for words, and her twin is the same. It is out of the ordinary to hear Elena talk, but she says more words than Enzel.

Vanora can count on one hand the times she has heard his voice since their first days together on assessment day, a day when Lixtis chooses who will be unit Captain and who will be with them for the remainder of their lifespans.

"I said what we were all thinking. He did not take too kindly to it." Vanora keeps any expression from her face as she speaks. She has never troubled her unit with the problems she faces daily. To them, they only know that she is their master's go-to for information and comradery. It is none of their business what else goes on behind closed doors.

Enzel's blue eyes are stuck on the side of her face from his spot by his twin sister. She knows he can barely see the purple staining her face from his position, but it does not stop him from boring a hole in her skin with his assessing eyes.

"It is no one's concern from this point forward how or when I get bruises. We are about to walk into a war, and we are all going to bear the scars of that. Make this no different."

"Yes, Captain." They all say in unison.

"Now, go pack a bag. We need to be on our way; they are already expecting us. Lixtis has informed the watch on duty of our arrival." She continues straight down the hall where they all walk together as her unit opens the doors on either side of her to enter their rooms.

Vanora takes a breath as she cracks her neck with her hands, instantly releasing some of the stress from her muscles. The movement only adds to the soreness building in the fibers of her neck from Lixtis's shove earlier.

A trip away from Souls Haven will do her some good, but not as much as cutting down the Demonians.

4

BASHTIAN

Making the morning rounds of the camp has become Bashtian's new routine. He wakes up before daybreak, gets dressed in his Captain's garments, pulls on his boots, and then makes his way around the outskirts of the tents.

He keeps a mental checklist of each one and how many warriors or healers call their pitched pieces of fabric home. Some tents even house small families since the time between the waves of battle has become further with each passing one. The vacant space gives the Demonians plenty of time to warm each other's beds, which produces enough children that Mariem now oversees not only healing but teaching.

Bashtian is aware of the knowledge the woman holds because she has taught him a lot of what he uses daily. The only difference is that he was never a child. He was created only as a man.

A man that had to learn like a child but with the ability to retain knowledge like a scholar such as Mariem. It was the same for

Mariem, but she was made with the ability to heal where Bashtian was gifted the ability of shadows and death.

It is what makes him one of the strongest of his race and the most respected. It helps that he is kind and courteous. Bashtian savored the moments making his rounds around the tents. The laughter of the children and the wails of the babes make him think that one day he will have what everyone around him has.

A family.

He has had his share of women and men to warm his bed, but none of them are what he needs. They have come and gone just like the moon does with the sun or an insect to a corpse.

Neither stays for longer than they are needed, nor do they stay once they've taken all they can. Bashtian hopes his person is out there somewhere, and thanks to Etbris, he hopes he will know the feeling. The God has made sure that each of them knows what it is to love and be loved.

"Bashtian, having a peaceful walk for your morning round this morning?" Mariem stands in front of him by the time he makes eye contact with her. Zoe stands by her side with their fingers interlocked.

"Good morning, Mariem." Bashtian lightly bows his head as he says their names. "Zoe."

"Good morning, Captain." Zoe returns the bow just before she brings a steaming cup of dark liquid to her mouth.

"It has been nice. A little quiet but nice." Bashtian places his hands inside the pockets of his coat. His eyes wander around the forest before he looks back at Mariem and her wife.

"When do you think we can expect to see Battlements again?" Zoe asks as her cup leaves her mouth. Mariem only stares at Bashtian as he looks between them both.

"Etbris said we need to be there at daybreak tomorrow." Bashtian's expression becomes serious as he relays the information to their best medical assistant and the Captain directly under him in rank.

Zoe nods her shaved head as she takes another sip of her warm drink. It does not surprise Bashtian at how she reacts; Zoe has seen many battles and even more deaths. She gives any competitor a challenge with her ability to disappear and reappear out of thin air.

"Sounds good, Captain. I will see you there." He watches as she turns to go back inside the couple's tent, but before Zoe walks away, she places a hand on Mariem's right cheek and gently turns her wife's head to place a kiss on her lips.

Bashtian is envious of the act but does not let it show on his face. He has hidden his loneliness from the people around him because they are content with their lives. Each one has someone to call their own, or they are comfortable having a revolving door into their living quarters. Bashtian only wants to know what it feels like to have someone that loves him like Zoe does Mariem. Lust is a feeling that only lasts for a moment, and he wants something that lasts for a lifetime.

Mariem smiles at her wife just before Zoe leaves them to greet the morning sun. Bashtian is happy that Mariem has a reason to smile so much, but he wishes he had the same.

"I take it you will be joining my wife on the front lines tomorrow?" Mariem asks with assessing eyes.

"Yeah, I am." Bashtian keeps his answer simple because he knows where the conversation is headed.

Mariem nods her head. "Mm-hmm, well then, I guess I need to ask you to look out for her."

Bashtian grins as he shakes his head. "Is it really that hard to ask me a favor without having to assess me and then say it like a jab?"

"Actually, yes, it is. I am not someone that is comfortable asking for help, and when it comes to my wife, I never like to think of a time when she will not make it back to me." Mariem's eyes develop a dark cast over them. It is one Bashtian has seen plenty of times. It is a distant look that shows the lengths someone will go for someone they love. Someone they cannot live without.

Bashtian removes his hand out of his pocket and gently sets it on Mariem's shoulder before giving it a light squeeze. "Mariem, you know I will always look after Zoe."

Her face relaxes with his words, but Bashtian does not feel as relaxed as she does. The pressure to keep everyone in this camp safe weighs on him, but he would rather die than leave them to face another battle alone.

He guesses that is why Etbris made him the way he did.

With a swift nod of her head, Mariem gives his hand a soft pat just before turning back into her tent. The tight bun on her head seems to sparkle from the morning light as it catches the gel Bashtian has seen her slather on her head to make sure none of the black hairs stray from their place.

It always makes him feel delighted to think about how simple a person can be when looking at Mariem. She never fixes her hair any other way; in fact, the only thing that changes about her is the color of dress she chooses. Even then, it is never anything other than her basic palette of light neutrals.

Zoe, on the other hand, is completely different from her. She changes her hair anytime it grows to a reasonable length. The last time it was long enough to grab, she asked Matryles, one of their closest friends, to shave it down to her scalp. Her reasoning was that it was too tedious to maintain.

Mariem does not mind that her partner changes her looks as often as she can change her clothes, but Bashtian thinks that is what makes them perfect for each other. One is fine with simplicity and the other spontaneity.

As he continues his walk, Bashtian cannot help but marvel at the beauty of the area surrounding them.

Etbris's army settled on the lower part of Baith, one of the seven islands that make up The Hatly Cluster. The area is surrounded by dense forest with heavy tree canopy that offers perfect coverage from anything flying above. The island is also the second-closest point to Death's Keep, Etbris's home.

The location was picked out specifically for that reason. Etbris wanted them to be someplace where he could relay messages easier than if they were on the far side of The Hatly Cluster.

The trees all shoot straight up to the sky like arrows. Their bright green leaves never waver from their spot on the branches, even though the wind puts up a fight with its breeze.

A small creek flows between the trunks of the trees like a snake, filtered by miles of different-sized pebbles and rocks, giving them the perfect drinking water. The soft sounds of the current find a way to relax anything that sits by it, often allowing the visitors to fall into a deep slumber. If it were not for that creek, which the army named Cleansing Creek, they would have to source their water straight from Tamsomin, the sea that surrounds everything in Arugo. Cleaning the water of salt would take days, but thanks to Cleansing Creek, they do not have the added hassle.

Birds and other small wildlife fly or run about in their camp. The bigger game tends to shy away, but what can you expect when all they smell is their kind or others like them being roasted over the open flames of a fire? Bashtian supposes it is their instinct to hide from a place consumed by the death of their own, but it is a feeling he does not possess. His feet are about to step upon a field that is tarnished by the blood of his people, their bodies consumed by the earth. The feeling of walking on top of Demonians he has known since their creation will haunt him until the last breath leaves his lungs.

After giving the area one last look, Bashtian decides he needs to find some sustenance to fuel his body before he calls for a meeting to go over the plans for tomorrow's fight.

For some reason that he cannot put his finger on, Bashtian feels like this battle will be one of significance. He hopes that if his gut is correct, it is not because of anything bad.

II

BONDS ARE TESTED

1,297 A.B.

5

VANORA

The flight from Souls Haven to Lorenon was not her favorite due to the amount of wind they had to fight through, but they made it to the rest of the Astrial Army. None of which thought of telling her how bad it smells here.

The land of Lorenon reeks of mold and mud. The region is encased by mountains, making it hard to navigate over the top due to the cloud coverage, but what makes it even worse is how the snow from the tips melts down into the land. Paired with the almost constant rainfall, it makes for a persistently water-logged region.

Vanora has been in their camp for a day and has already wanted to fly to Battlements just for a change of smell. The stench of rot would be more pleasurable to her nose than whatever curse has been inflicted on this ground.

Almost immediately after their arrival, Lixtis echoed his orders into her mind. They where simple enough because all he demanded was that the Demonians feel the loss of their numbers like he has the Astrials. Lixtis wants the battlefield to be drenched in the blood of his brothers creations to remind Etbris of the power that he has.

She relayed the information to her unit and then spread the word to the rest of the army. Now, everyone is scurrying around to make sure their blades are sharpened and their white plate armor is polished.

"Nora, you need to eat before it is time to catch some shut eye." Quinnie shoves a bowl of stew towards her, but Vanora cannot bring herself to grab it.

Something does not feel right inside of her. It is not the feeling of impending doom, because Vanora has felt that often in her life, especially since being the main one under Lixtis's thumb. This feeling she can only describe as uncertainty because, for the first time in her life, she does not know what her body is trying to tell her.

Her face is expressionless as she looks at Quinnie, who sits to her right, her eyes cast to the fire as she shovels her own bowl of stew into her mouth. Her discarded bowl sits unbothered between them.

As the glow of the flames dance over her friend's face, Vanora cannot help but think of how beautiful she is. The contrast between her light brown hair and sun-kissed skin makes her someone worthy of having a portrait painted.

Quinnie must feel Vanora's honey brown eyes on the side of her face because she turns her head and smiles at Vanora, who does not return the gesture. Forcing the expression from her lips when it does not feel genuine is not something Vanora will do. The unknown feeling rising inside of her makes her soak in this moment, just studying her friend's face. If this is the last time she sets eyes upon Quinnie then she wants to make sure every detail is memorized.

"I do not think I have ever told you this, but you are very beautiful, and I am glad that you are my friend." Vanora watches as her friend, with chestnut brown eyes with an inner halo of green that seems to burst from the iris like an exploding star, slowly stops chewing her food.

Vanora does not know why she says this to Quinnie, but if the feeling building inside of her is due to her instincts knowing tomorrow will not go well, she wants to make sure her right-hand woman knows how much she appreciates her.

Quinnie swallows her food as she says, "Now, do not go getting all sappy on me just because we have a war to fight in tomorrow. We will see each other before, during, and after." Her hand gives Vanora's shoulder a slap as her mouth turns into a crooked smile. This time Vanora matches it as she hangs her head just before grabbing her stew from its spot between them.

"Yeah, well, now you know." Vanora begins to shovel spoonfuls of meat and gravy into her mouth as Elena and Enzel take their seats to the left side of the fire.

In silence, the four Astrial Angels that make up the main unit of the God of Souls' army eat their stew and watch the flames of the fire dance in the center of them.

Tomorrow will come in the blink of an eye for them all, but only one of them will be left shaken to their core by news they never thought they would learn about themselves.

6

BASHTIAN

Bashtian watches as the army of Demonians assumes their positions around the open field of Battlements. The land under his black armor-clad feet is drained of life. There is no grass, flowers, insects, or trees.

It is no more than a barren wasteland accustomed to the sounds of the wounded and dying. The only thing making it feel like a field made of dirt and minerals are the various sized hills that make for an uneven fighting terrain.

Every warrior around him is silent as their eyes search the clear, open, blue sky above them; only a few scattered clouds fill the void of blue as they wait for the arrival of their opponent.

He can feel the added strength coursing through each of the warriors from his presence being among them.

The camp had been in constant chatter about his arrival, and how he would add another barrier between them and death. When his name is spoken from their mouths, it is met with high regards.

Bashtian stands tall at the front lines of his God's army with the knowledge that he was created for this. His job as a protector is to defend every innocent life that he encounters. No matter what wings grace their back or lack thereof. Bashtian will safeguard those that need it.

The ones that do not will meet their fate by either his broadsword or one of his warriors. Their death will come quickly if he has it his way, but he cannot say the same if anyone else gets to them first. He does not control anyone's actions but his own.

The Eternal War has caused mass casualties to both the Demonians and Astrials; he thinks their disdain for burying their friends is mutual though. No matter what anyone says.

The information has not left his head that most of the fallen Astrial Angels were all juveniles. Because of that, he took his time this morning, weeding out any warrior who was not the proper age to witness the bloodbath that would occur today. Bashtian only allowed those old enough to have more than four adult years of battle training to walk behind him. It caused a lot of anger from the younger Demonians, but they will understand one day.

If they live long enough to make a life for themselves that is not just training, battling, and dying, then he thinks he will have accomplished something great. Then those too young to sign their death papers now will have the time to understand why he would not let them stand on this field with him today. If he lives on for another hundred years and the battle is not over, then they will get their time to fight under his name like they want to do so early in their lives.

Bashtian searches the slightly clouded sky for any sign of the Astrials, but his eyes only find the sparse number of clouds floating their way around the open space. His ears, on the other hand, do not miss the slight changes in pitch of the wind. The way its steady rhythm trails off to a broken, unpredictable tune is the first sign he needs to make his first call.

"Demonians!" Bashtian's deep tone seems to pulse towards the army with every ounce of command in his broad, built frame. It travels between each warrior, causing their attention to focus only on their Captain in front of them. As soon as he can feel every set of eyes on him, Bashtian turns his back to the open field. His black armor rattles with each of his movements.

"Stand ready." Without another word, everyone that makes up their hundreds' strong army adjusts their heads so that they all look straight ahead, their shoulders squared. The clashing of metal fills the air as their own black armor lets out a war cry with each of their movements.

"Eyes to the sky!" No other words need to be said as Bashtian turns back to face the open ground that awaits them.

Drawing his dark black broadsword, specially made by Etbris himself, Bastian looks to his right to ensure that his warriors are ready. Standing shoulder to shoulder beside him are his men, Zorro, Torrien, and Matryles. Looking over to his left, he locks eyes with Zoe and Hinchy. Everyone that means the most to him stands by his side on the front lines. With them, he knows he never has to look out for his own back; they all do well to keep each other alive.

Just as he places his shadowy brown eyes back towards the sky, they find a shining, bright light falling through a solo wandering cloud and surrounding it even more of the same burning light. Only those do not hold the same dominance as the one in the middle.

The sight makes his chest tighten and his teeth grind against themselves. He can feel each small black line begin to trail their way up his forearms and from the small wrinkles by the corner of his eyes.

Bashtian does not know if the Astrials know that he has come to be their one-way ticket to death, but he knows they will put up a fight either way.

As the lights get closer to the ground, the shape of their bodies begins to come into focus. A gasp comes from beside Bashtian, causing him to bring his attention to Zoe.

"What?" His voice is stern.

"That is Vanora." Zoe's words are quiet so that no one else can hear them, but no one else even knows what the first Angel looks like. Lixtis made sure she stayed hidden among the clouds and away from prying eyes. The way the God hides her is like when a child has a sweet their parent does not know about. He has always felt like Vanora was nothing more than a special toy that Lixtis would not risk getting broken or tainted by any outsider that is not himself.

Bashtian blows a breath from his nose just as a hard boom rattles the ground under their feet. Looking to the center of the field, he finds the source of the disturbance.

Standing at the head of the army is a woman wearing bright white armor with gold appliques. Her hair is tied back in a single plait, the sun making the red shine like a beacon. Bashtian must force himself to swallow to clear his dry throat as her warm brown eyes set in a scowl with the rest of her face. The wings made of pure white feathers that fan out on full display behind her make her seem like she could be a Goddess. She does not wear the white cloth like most of the younger warriors adorn. It shows that the understanding she has for her powers is greater than the ones that wear theirs.

Bashtian knows firsthand that it can take the Astrials hundreds of years to control the simmering light inside themselves to go without their cloth. It makes him sad to think that most of them never see the world with their own eyes before they meet their death, but it does make their other senses excellent.

The clothed ones only reveal their eyes when they need the upper hand in battle, but the ones that do not have them can use their light at any time. That makes them deadly on the field because who can dodge a blow of scorching light fired from an enemy who also fights another? The shots will come out of nowhere and be gone before anyone's eyes can adjust to know which Astrial sent them out. Many of the Demonians have fallen because of their light, their bodies charred, and left void of all organs.

The rustling of wings from behind him draws Bashtian from the trance the woman in front of him has on him. Squaring his shoulders and splaying his dark tan flesh color wings out behind him, Bashtian holds his head high as he says, "Demonians, creations of the God of Death, Etbris. We fight! We protect! We serve! Leave no one to die alone!"

As those words fill the ears of each Demonian, the army behind him hoists their blades towards the sky as they release their battle cry.

"We fight! We protect! We serve! Leave no one to die alone!"

Bashtian angles the blade of his sword parallel with the ground just before he gives the handle a light twirl in the palm of his hand. From across the way, they hear an answering cry.

"Show no mercy! Kill the weakened! Destroy the abominations!"

Before Bashtian can comprehend what the growing ache in his chest means or if his friends are ready, the Astrial Angels launch half of themselves into the sky as the other half begins their charge on foot.

7

VANORA

Vanora watches from her spot as the massive Demonian Captain makes sure each of his warriors is going where he needs them to. He directs the left flank to the furthest hill on their side. The right launches into the sky without any other commands than his black sword being thrust upward; center mass breaks around him and separates half to the right, the rest to the center of the field. Vanora does not miss that five warriors stay by his side until the very last minute.

Her own army begins to make their way towards the others in no particular order because they know where they need to be and when they need to get there. The structure of their movements is meant to cause confusion, making the others feel like they have no guidance. Vanora wastes none of her energy moving. She stays in the same spot she has been standing in since they landed.

She will never be the first one to run into combat; no true leader would. If something were to happen to her, who would take the reins in this war? That is the question she asks herself, and the only thing she can give herself to make her body stay where it is. With the adrenaline coursing its way through her veins, it takes every ounce of strength she has not to launch herself into the middle of the bloodshed. She is needed for this war; an early death from a split second decision could be the end to her kind.

It is hard for her to watch as blood begins to rain down from the cloudless sky along with echoes of swords clashing becoming an offbeat rhythm with her heart. Each beat in her chest is half a second off from the collision of metal. The sound of metal is a quarter of a second from the sound of screams. Her people's bodies fall from the sky, but they are often tangled with those of Demonians.

Vanora does not feel anything for the ones falling around her, but as a leader, she will give her life to make sure that her people are safe. Even if they think of her as their master's whore.

As the chaos of battle grips its ragged claws into everyone around her, Vanora looks to the Captain of the Demonians, who can only be the one and only Bashtian. She knows it is true because all his characteristics are just as Lixtis had described.

He radiates power and dominance, whereas all the others do not. Their energy gives off many different things: bravery, nervousness, anger, but none of them are as potent as his commanding aura. The markings on his armor are a tell-tell sign of someone with more importance than any run-of-the-mill Demonian. Much like hers breaks her apart from the rest of her army.

They are both symbols of this war. They are both martyrs.

Vanora has not let his constant stares go unnoticed as her scowl for him deepens. She has been taught that everything these things stand for is the opposite of what Lixtis wants. Her God and master wants what his brother took from him when they were first made together in the Nether, a space of nothingness where only Light and Shadow reside laying side by side.

She recites the tale told to her as her eyes stay locked onto the solid black ones looking directly at her.

When Light created Lixtis, the power made sure that everything pure was compressed into the shell of a single body. It wanted its son to be powerful. Strong. Someone that shared the same thoughts and aspirations as itself.

Lixtis said that when Shadow made his smaller brother, Light got angry at its love. It did not want anything that could dim the brightness of the perfect son it had just made from a fiber of itself.

Shadow did not see Lixtis as such. The darkness tried to make Light believe that her master had greed growing inside of his chest, where his heart should rest. It is why it gave a part of itself to Etbris instead of Lixtis, like Light had wanted it to.

Now, Lixtis spends his time trying to get the power that his brother stole from him from the very beginning. Shadow's choice to build another instead of giving its essence to Lixtis caused him to have to fight for it back. That power has not been used to the ability that it is meant for but instead used to make a mockery of everything that Lixtis is.

As Bashtian gets closer and the screams begin to engulf the field, Vanora draws her shining sword from its sheath. Time seems to slow as the Demonian gets closer to her, and a slight pain begins to hammer in her chest as the distance between them closes.

Vanora has no idea where the members of her unit are, and she cannot bring herself to look for them. Not when the look of the man walking closer to her makes her face slacken slightly.

Lost are her thoughts of disgust for these people as this one man finds a way to take her breath from her lungs. The darkness of his eyes does not make her think any less of him, nor do the black vein-like lines currently running down his face. She grips her sword tighter in her hand as he stops short of being directly in her space.

Vanora can feel his eyes moving over each different plate of armor as the sound of the dying slowly begins to fade from around her. All she can hear is each breath he takes and the way his heart beats a little too fast for it to be caused by his adrenaline alone.

"Vanora." Her name leaving his lips makes the pain in her chest grow. The cadence of his voice mixed with the depth of his husky tone makes her straighten herself even more than she already was. It feels like his voice alone can take her down by the knees.

"Bashtian." She has no idea why she says his name, but the small smirk that the warrior tries to hide tells her that she has his full attention.

"Let's have some fun," Vanora says as she raises her sword in a flash and brings it down towards Bashtian's head.

A low chuckle meets her ears just before her swing is stopped by a black sword laced in smoke. Irritation blooms inside of her at the blocked swing, which brings the fighter in her to the surface. Even the velvet-laced way her name sounds coming from between his teeth cannot save him from her now.

If he wants a fight, then she will give him one. Before another word can be shared between them, the pair meets each other blow for blow in the middle of her army and his friends.

The only distraction she faces with each dodge of his swing is the new beat deep inside of her chest, and with each new beat comes a layer of confusion. The thoughts of killing the man in front of her, her sworn enemy, have come to a halt. She only wishes she knew why.

8

BASHTIAN

With each block of his sword, Bashtian cannot seem to take his eyes from the warrior in front of him. The woman he swore to defeat as soon as he saw her, now playing with him like he is a babe. He should be tearing her limb from limb, letting the darkness in his soul feast on the light in her. Instead, he is enjoying watching her facial expressions change with each failed swing.

He knows he is in the middle of a war with hundreds of his friends around him. They need a protector at this very moment, but they are not getting that from him. The way Vanora looks like a glowing crystal in the shining sun seems to take all his common sense from him.

Etbris has explained that when Lixtis created Vanora, he wanted to make someone that would make any living thing stop in their tracks. He created her as something to parade around and show off. The thought makes Bashtian angry because the woman in front of him, who currently launches herself into the sky with him hot on her trail, is so much more than a prize to be flaunted. She is filled with power, and from the way he can see each passing thought move across her eyes, Bashtian knows she is filled with knowledge.

He does not know Vanora, but Bashtian can feel in his heart that she is innocent of her master's wrongdoings. The beating organ in his chest has never led him astray before, and he has no reason not to trust it now.

As they continue their battle above the ground, Bashtian finally breaks his gaze from the pretty face in front of him. He needs to find Zoe and see how she is holding her wing of the army.

Luckily, she is not hard to find due to her ability to transport anywhere she needs with just a simple thought or mental image of the place she is going.

It comforts Bashtian that she is holding her own and that his time being distracted has not caused her to fall. He is not sure how long Vanora and himself have been lost in each other's movements, but as the sound of battle cries fills his ears, he cannot stop the fact that they are in the middle of a war.

He is the commander of the Demonian army and she of the Astrials.

Two lifelong enemies that share none of the same goals at the end of the day. If it were not for her striking beauty and swift moves with a sword, then he does not think he would have looked twice at her.

The ache blossoming in his chest says otherwise, though.

A warm substance begins to seep from his armor just as his eyes begin to roam the grounds for any of his other close friends. Looking to his right shoulder, Bashtian notices that his skin glows a dull shade of white.

Vanora has managed to nick his shoulder just under the connective fibers of the metal. Looking at his competitor, Bashtian expects to see her face full of pride for getting a blow on him. To his shock, the opposite is written in her features. What he finds is a look of worry mixed with concern. Her sword is raised to the side of her head like she is about to deliver another strike, but it is frozen in its spot.

Bashtian looks back to his injury before looking back at Vanora.

"That was a lucky hit. I bet you will not get another one." A smile does not develop on his face, but he uses his words to reassure that he is okay.

Never has he thought that he would meet Vanora on the battlefield and be sending her words of reassurance after she caused him to bleed.

His eyes catch the small bob of her throat as she lowers her sword slightly. "I caught you when you were distracted." Her voice sounds eternal in his ears, and her words hold true. He was distracted, but not as much as he had been with her on this field cloaked by death.

As her sword lowers another inch, Bashtian raises his enough to bring it down towards her own shoulder. With a flash, he separates the skin underneath the connecting parts of metal like she did to him. No noise leaves her lips as she accepts her punishment.

"There, now we are even," Bashtian says as they begin to circle each other. Their warriors fight below and above them, many already laying on the ground.

"Yeah, I guess so." Vanora watches him with a closeness he has never seen before, her nose taking small sniffs of the air. He can smell everything about her, making his senses only able to focus on her. It makes him weak in a way he has never been before. He tells himself he needs to finish the job at hand so that no one else must die.

If only it was that easy.

This encounter has added a new element that he did not expect, and right now, if you asked him to kill Vanora, he could not do it.

He would be a failure, and for the first time in his long life, he would be content with it.

9

ETBRIS

Taking a walk around his palace, Etbris can feel the winds changing and, with it, what flows through their wisdom-packed filaments. Each one whispering a different piece of information past his ears.

He does not have to listen closely to know that his top warrior, and Captain of his army, has met the person that is meant for him. The person that everyone only dreams of finding, especially when it is another race outside of their own. Truth be told, the God knew it was a chance he would take if he sent Bashtian to the front lines, but Zoe needed a break.

The unknown of the situation makes his stomach feel uneasy. By telling himself that it is something they will deal with when the time comes, even though he already knows what must be done, eases some of the strain.

He will not hesitate to send word to Bashtian to meet with him about the matter. Besides, what else is there to do when the one person that is in control of your army is falling for the Captain of your brothers?

The enemy.

As he continues his walk around his home, Etbris is met by one of the Shadow Hounds that oversee bringing the deceased souls to their home until they are chosen to be reborn into another form. This hound is only one of the few that has stayed around Death's Keep while the rest of their pack have long since left to find whatever it is they are missing.

Placing a hand on the top of the hound's head, he cannot help but to take a deep breath for stability.

The conversation with Bashtian will not be easy, but it is needed. The Eternal War has been fought for too long and needs to come to an end. If that means his number one Demonian becomes the husband to an Astrial Angel, then so be it. Anything is better than what they are facing right now.

Etbris just hopes that nothing is done that can cause even more uproar than they are already dealing with when it comes to Lixtis.

His brother does not see any of his creations as anything more than property. They are his own personal toys to use and torture. The older God often reminds his little brother of the children who would lie to get the attention they needed from their parents.

As Etbris thinks about it, the comparison is true. Since the day they were born from the fabric of Light and Shadow, Lixtis has never seen him as an equal. To his older brother, Etbris has always been a mistake.

To a being like the God of Souls, the worst thing you can be seen as is a waste of space or competition. Etbris believes that if they had more time together, to know each other, then their relationship might be different. He never wanted to fight his brother. It is something that has always made Etbris unhappy, but he will not forgive Lixtis for the innocent lives he has taken.

The amount of misery he has put not only Etbris through but also everyone else he encounters is not something that can be mended with a simple apology. Every living thing on Arugo and Sytherac demands blood for blood. That is something he will not deny because he wants to see the life drain from his brother's eyes as well.

Etbris often dreams of what it will be like to finally watch his brother fall to his knees as the power of Light drains from his body, but it is not for his own pleasure. No, he dreams of the day so that every life that has been taken by Lixtis's hands can finally be repaid. Even though he knows it will not physically bring anything back from the depths of the darkness, the anticipation brings Etbris hope.

"A wrongful death is a soul wasted," Etbris says to himself. "A wasted soul is a heart yet to grow."

He does not notice that he is speaking into the empty space between him and the Shadow Hound, but Etbris does know that it can take a lifetime for a heart to fill the gaps inside of a being. It takes trial and error for anything to grow to the full potential that they deserve. When they do, it is the most extraordinary thing to witness. Lixtis has robbed so many of that opportunity, and all Etbris wants is to make sure they know that their death was not wasted by a God filled to the brim with hate.

The Shadow Hound, still waiting for his attention, nudges his thigh. Etbris brings himself from the turmoil he faces on the inside as he looks to the black pits of the hounds face.

"Am I needed, Fletcher?" The hound huffs softly at the sound of his name.

"Lead the way." Etbris gestures to the space down the corridor where he currently walks. Fletcher wastes no time as he hastens his trot by Etbris's side.

Fletcher has been one of the main transport hounds since the day he created the Shadow Hounds. He was not the first one made, but he was the first one that chose to stay by his creator's side like a best friend. Etbris has always liked the hound because something about him made him stand out from the rest. It is like he has an actual soul trapped tight in his shadow-filled chest, not just the power of the darkness like the others.

He is not bigger or stronger than his siblings because they can change their shape anyway they like; instead, Fletcher seems to listen. He listens like one of the Demonians. What Etbris says goes just as it does with the warriors, but not with the Shadow Hounds. This fact does not bother Etbris since he made them to be their own entities. He wanted them to find whoever they thought was greater than him, and when they left his home in search of that person, Etbris did not take it to heart.

He hopes someone out there can give the hounds what they are looking for. They can go where they please and return when they need to. All the hounds know they will always have a home at Death's Keep.

Fletcher is one of the few that have decided to stay at the palace in the darkness that covers the bottom of Arugo. The rest have gone their separate ways from Etbris, but he can still feel that they are in Arugo, silently helping the ones on the battlefield from the cover of the shadows. Even if none of the warriors know about their secret sidekicks.

"Do you think the others will find peace when they find someone they think is worthy?" Etbris strokes Fletcher's neck as he waits for an answer.

One does not come from the hound's snout but instead from the way the shadows begin to dance around his hand. Each different connection to his skin sends a small tingle up his arm. They feel like a warm hug, and for Fletcher, that means he is showing reassurance.

"I know you chose me as well as a handful of the others, but I worry about the ones who are still searching. It is not a nice feeling to be lost, constantly hunting for something and not knowing what it is. It can be debilitating." Another round of tingles rushes up his skin as they continue their walk to wherever Etbris is being guided.

He is about to ask where he is going but stops himself as they round a corner. In front of Etbris stand the doors to the kitchen. His nose is greeted with a wonderful smell that makes his mouth begin to water.

Taking his hand from Fletcher, Etbris does not wait to push his body through the doors to find what causes the lovely smell. He is not surprised to see a platter of fresh meats and vegetables laid out on top of the metal prep table in the middle of the kitchen. Etbris is not sure which chef prepared the meal for him, but he is grateful that they have. Hunger takes over him for the first time in days.

The task at hand has outweighed his need for sustenance until now. Placing his palms on the cool surface of the table, Etbris raises his body from the ground until he can easily swing his legs underneath himself.

As he positions himself so that he sits comfortably, Fletcher finds his spot on the floor by the kitchen's entrance. Etbris wastes no time bringing the tray of food in front of him just before he dives in.

The list of tasks he must fulfill, along with the conversations, fades away in the moments that he fuels his body until the next time he gets a free moment. Tomorrow will come and bring on the same set of challenges, so he allows himself to enjoy peace in the moments that he has it.

III

FORBIDDEN BONDS

1,299 A.B.

THE DAYS SINCE LIXTIS SENT VANORA OFF TO BATTLEMENTS HAVE been bleak. Jackal is not doing for him what he has become used to while with Vanora, and the man's constant cries give the God severe headaches. He has thought about retracting her punishment so he has her company again, but then he would look weak.

Lixtis has never allowed himself to look weak. He will not start now, especially when it comes to something as degrading as needing a companion. He has a constant supply of bodies that he can choose from, but he always goes back to her.

He is only possessive of her, only protective over her.

Well, as protective as one can be when they only genuinely care for themselves, the wellbeing of a favorite belonging is another thing that can cause a person such as himself to act the way he does with Vanora. *His* Vanora, only his.

No updates have been sent to him about the war besides the usual body count of the slain. None of which have had her name, so he has not given them more than a once over. Lixtis could care less who lives or dies on that battlefield if they remember their Laws and who created them. Those two things are good enough for him.

After all, when an Astrial Angel dies, their power flows back into his veins, so he does not really lose anything. Unlike his little brother, who chooses to let the power of darkness release back into the minerals of their soil.

Lixtis has always seen it as a waste of power, but no matter how many bodies drain the black substance from their veins into the barren field of Battlements, Etbris does not seem to be affected by the loss. He can still feel the vibrations of his brother's power even all the way in the clouds.

The sheer force it must take for something to stretch its way into the safety of Souls Haven, causing Lixtis the slightest bit of unease, is the type of thing the God craves.

What he does gain to lose is the distance he has gained towards Etbris and the darkness that he carries. That power that should have been his is being wasted in the body of someone like his brother. No one as tenderhearted and quiet as Etbris can truly wield such a power like that from Shadow. The ultimate ability would be to be able to not only create life but destroy it with only a blink of an eye. To hold all that energy inside of his soul and take the spots of Light and Shadow is what Lixtis dreams of; it is all he can imagine.

Sitting on his throne, Lixtis finds himself twirling a curl around his fingertip, compiling what his next move should be. Jackal has been dismissed for the day because Lixtis found that the beast's obsessive whining triggers his already heated temper. The last thing he wants to do is worry about his pearl white floor being stained by blood yet again. It took the Wingless two weeks to restore the floor of the palace the last time one of the warriors thought it was a clever idea to question his war tactics.

The Wingless are the few chosen caretakers that make sure the cleanliness of Souls Haven stays its sparkling white color, given the name because, to Lixtis, they do not need any other. They chose their path the day they decided to conspire with Etbris in the beginning of The Eternal War. Only he decided to take their wings and make them live out the rest of their Angelic lives scrubbing his floors. They should thank him for his mercilessness for the crime they have committed; he did spare their lives when he decided not to cast them down to Sytherac.

Lixtis is sure that his brother's carefully divided world is more tortuous than the basic task of scrubbing the perfectly carved floor of Souls Haven.

Lixtis blames them and every other Angel that has tried to step on his toes and for every blood splatter that has stained his home. He would not have to murder so many of them if they all learned how to listen and obey, like Vanora.

It seems like all his thoughts always focus back on the female Astrial Angel; it is not how he thought it would be when he first created her. Instead of another body to use and disregard, he has made her the leader of his army and the warmth that shares his bed when no one else can.

Lixtis knows that she holds a vast amount of power in his mind, but he cannot untether himself from her. He has thought of unusual ways to do it more times than he would like to count or share out loud. When lost in his thoughts about Vanora, it is the only time he feels shame. The feeling is not for how he treats her but for how he has let her infiltrate the inner workings of his frontal lobe.

Lixtis has never allowed a nuisance like Vanora to stay trapped inside of his walls, but there has never been anything like the woman before.

To him, she is someone to lock away out of fear of the power she has over him.

To her, he is just someone that she must obey or risk dying.

Lixtis knows how she feels even if she does not say it, but what she does not understand is that he has given her grace. He has given her countless chances to give herself to him willingly. Something that has never happened. It is why he resorts to commanding her, because no Angel can deny a command from their master. Not even the very first one created that holds a special place in his dark and twisted mind. He will soon break one of his own laws, but he is a God. The laws do not apply to him.

That is why Lixtis has already decided that after Vanora comes back from the punishment, he will wed her, and they will create something that is more powerful than anything Etbris can fathom.

A low chuckle rises from the God's throat as his eyes press close and a smile plasters itself across his face, revealing two rows of perfectly polished teeth.

"Nothing will stop the power that I create with her. She will carry a babe strong enough to bring any God to their knees." Lixtis opens his eyes as he takes a moment to contemplate the next words before they break free of his lips, knowing that he could be sealing his fate with two small words, "including me."

His head rests back against his throne as images of his perfectly crafted warlord begin to manifest in perfect bloody detail.

The God has never dreamed of creating a biological offspring, but that is what he needs to win this war against his brother, to gain him better access to Light and Shadow in the Nether.

Another weapon to teach.

Another to control.

Another to dispose of after the war is won.

11

VANORA

IT FEELS LIKE AN ETERNITY HAS BEEN WASTED ON THE SOIL OF Battlements. Vanora left every fight with only minor wounds to show. It has become her and Bashtian's custom since the first time they could not end each other while standing toe to toe. The twin cuts from one of the only times they willingly harmed each other have healed into matching scars. They will be a constant reminder of the first time in her life she showed an enemy mercy.

Lixtis has not called her back to Souls Haven, so the time at Lorenon has become her new normal. Vanora can freely walk around camp without the other warriors looking at her as if she is a myth. She cannot blame them for their assessing glazes when she first arrived. Vanora would stare at something that she thought was nothing more than a made up dream by someone powerful enough to wage a war like the one they are forced to fight.

The time away from the palace has reminded her that being an Astrial Angel is not bad when you are away from prying eyes. It has also given her time to try to understand the reason why she cannot bring herself to kill Bashtian, instead repeatedly sparing his life.

No matter how hard she tries to make her muscles cooperate with what she knows they need to do, they do not obey. The fight against herself is never won when she is faced with him. Something about him calls to an unknown part of her. It makes her second-guess every instinct and drives her to do unspeakable acts. Like following a Demonian Captain into the thicket of the forest to wash the dirt from his black armor. Or even going as far as weaving a thread and needle through his torn flesh to seal up a perfectly straight slice given to him by her own blade.

Bashtian did not say anything to Vanora the first night she followed him. Instead, he gently took the supplies from her hand, cleaned them, and then began to stitch up the cut his own sword caused her. Vanora could not do anything but watch his facial expressions as he worked the needle through each different layer of cut flesh. She will never forget how his dark eyebrows pulled in on themselves as small wrinkles graced the ridge of his nose from his concentration. The black veins that once covered his skin's surface left to their hiding place, exposing who he is underneath. Vanora did not speak a word that night either. Words would ruin the peace they both felt in the moment and the ones after when they sat by the small creek until daybreak.

The visits have remained their most precious secret, and for Vanora, something about those nights by that small creek seems like something more than she can describe. She thinks that is why her body drives her to keep going back, because she needs to discern the feeling taking over her body. It has become miserable to be in her skin during the day because of the questions she has to shove down until they make themselves known by the time the moon greets the sky.

Vanora never questioned who she was until her eyes locked with that damn Demonian warrior standing in front of his friends with his shoulders squared. The darkest brown eyes locked with hers, and flesh-covered wings flexed behind his back.

No one has questioned her about why Bashtian is not already dead, but Vanora can feel that some may be watching her with assessing eyes due to her lack of kills on the battlefield. It is something she must figure out the next time they are due back for another conflict. That is another problem she faces, because Vanora cannot strike down any of the Demonians. The thought of killing one of the enemy warriors makes her stomach feel like it will fall out of her. How can she take the life of someone who resembles her secret friend? It makes her feel like she would be killing him, and that is something she will not do.

Vanora sits next to the morning fire she made not even an hour ago. No one else stirs around her as she lets herself get lost in the overflowing amount of thoughts. Each one feels like it takes a nibble out of her already drained energy supply. Sleep has been something she has lacked since setting foot in Lorenon, but it has become a stranger for her more lately.

The mixing of the yellow and orange of the flames fuels her body with a tingling warmth as she lets her walls fall. As soon as they do, her mind is released from the vice grip of stress. In its place, she finds a carefully curated, made-up image of what Bashtian looks like underneath his heavy suit of armor. Vanora knows what she is doing is enough to get her executed in front of every single Angel that has been sculpted by Lixtis, but each night spent with the enemy is breaking down every piece of who she thought she was.

All regard to the Law of Angels has been tossed to the side as the image makes her skin feel like it is being touched by small waves of electricity. To her displeasure, it does not stop those fucking sentences from crossing her mind.

"No Angel is to breed outside of their own race. To do so means termination of the female and the abomination which she carries."

Luckily, the words leave her before they can plant themselves inside of her.

It only leaves the sensation room to take back over. It is something Vanora could get used to because nothing has caused a reaction like this before. Every nerve ending seems to be sparking at the same time, fitting together like a puzzle. For once, she thinks that her body might know how to act normally.

When she thought about herself before, all she saw was a thing to be owned. Something that was made to be nothing more than a beautiful object. To obey one master, never think for itself or understand what pleasure truly is. The body Vanora has been made into has only felt the touch of a vengeful, rough man who would rather take from her than ask and wait for her to give it. She has always been something for the taking to Lixtis, and for the first time, Vanora wants to have a say in what happens to her.

No more bruises given to her by bored hands.

No more sly smiles by a person who finds pleasure in her pain.

No more staying silent while she watches the people she cares for become nothing more than skeletons to rot away in the dirt, pecked away at by black birds of death.

The slight scrape of wood against wood draws Vanora's eyes up and to her left. There she finds Elena walking out of her small wooden home. It is a simple square cottage that the twins made after getting tired of sleeping on the damp soil of Lorenon. It did not surprise her because most of the warriors here have traded in their tents for wooden houses with thick sod roofs over their heads.

Vanora has stuck with her basic fabric shelter. The only luxury she has is the slightly raised wooden platform that keeps her from staying soaked by the constantly watered ground. Bashtian told her that his people have also decided to make their ground a home instead of a camp, except for him.

They share the same feeling about building something that could be silent without anyone to share it with. The heartbreak is not worth the comfort. Until Vanora has met someone worth making herself feel comfortable with, she will not be building anything permanent.

"How did you sleep?" Vanora asks Elena quietly as she takes a seat to her left.

"I think that is the hardest I have slept since leaving the palace." Elena's words are almost nonexistent over the crackle of the fire, but Vanora hears them. She has grown accustomed to using all her hearing strength when her softly-spoken friend chooses her words.

"Oh, yeah. Why is that?" She does not care to know the truth, but it seems like Elena is in the mood to talk this morning. Vanora can tell by the way her back straightens and her hands smooth out invisible wrinkles on her loose trousers. Words make the twins uncomfortable, and only one will voice them aloud. So, Vanora will enjoy the time Elena lets her hear her voice. Besides, you do not deny someone like Elena words when they come so sparsely.

A small smile blooms on Elena's thin lips just before Vanora corrects her hunched posture to match the woman sitting beside her.

"I had company," a slight hesitancy follows before she continues, "last night." Elena's face seems like it is glowing from the effect of her smile now. "It was the best time I have had in a long time, and afterward I slept like the dead."

Vanora grins as she listens to her friend giggle. The expression on Vanora's face soon starts to melt away as pain starts to build in her middle. She has never felt what Elena is feeling now, and the part of her that did not care before is slowly dissolving from existence.

"Should I ask who the lucky man was?" The question has no emotion tied to it, and Vanora looks back at the fighting flames to try and make it not seem noticeable.

"You cannot tell Enzel. I mean it, Nora. He would have my head if he knew." Elena positions herself so that she is facing Vanora, but all she gets is a slight nod in return. "It was Soran."

Vanora slowly turns her head to face Elena as the name leaves her mouth.

She is met with dark blue eyes that scream for Vanora to keep her voice quiet as she speaks. "You slept with your brother's best friend?" Her head tilts slightly as she gives Elena a once-over.

"Enzel is going to kill him when he finds out, Lena. You better hope that does not happen."

"I know, Nora. I know. That is why you cannot tell him." Elena grabs her hand as her words become slightly faster. "I did not mean for it to happen, but he has changed so much since he and Enzel first became friends. Soran makes me feel like a real woman. He does not question my strength like every other one has, and he made sure I was satisfied before he was."

Vanora does not move but instead searches Elena's eyes. What she finds makes the pain inside of her become almost unbearable because she has never known what true pleasure is. To her, it seems like something imaginary, but the way the eyes of her friend are filled with the possibilities of her future makes Vanora realize that it is not something made up. It is just something she has never experienced.

"I will take it to my grave. You have my word." Before Elena can say anything else, Vanora gives her hand a pat and rises from her spot on the log where she had rested. Not another word is said to her as she walks away from the fire.

She cannot bring herself to wrestle with everything going on inside of her and listen to how amazing it is to feel a man's touch that is not filled with menace. As she makes her way past the last of the wooden homes, Vanora spreads her wings and leaps into the blue sky still separating itself from the cast of the morning sun. If she does not understand what is going on in her body, she needs to ask someone who will not judge her. Someone who can explain it to her in a way that she will understand.

Vanora needs Bashtian. So, she will go find him.

Bashtian has not left his spot by Cleansing Creek since Vanora left him before sunrise. He found a spot at the very end where the filtered water runs back into the salty embrace of Tamsomin. No one has seen them together except on the battle-field. Bashtian does not think any of the others will understand what he is doing, and he cannot blame them. Sometimes *he* does not even know what he is doing. Especially after their last visit, because it took everything in him not to take Vanora's face in his hands and press her lips to his.

Their night was spent talking about the differences between their creators. Vanora is just getting used to the idea of sharing anything about Lixtis with him, but he only gives her the truth about Etbris. He likes telling stories of his life with Etbris and all the other Demonians, so sharing them with Vanora seems like he is sharing more of himself than he could imagine sharing with anyone else that is not a part of his unit.

He often catches the small grins that would try to become full smiles during some of his tales, but his enemy is excellent at shielding her emotions. It makes him think about some of the things Vanora has been through and whose hands dealt the punishment. He has an idea, but she has not told him herself. Until she does, Bashtian will not let his mind take him to such conclusions.

Shifting his legs, Bashtian brings his knees up to use as an armrest, and he cannot help but to think about the next time he will get to see her warm brown, honey-colored eyes. Vanora's face has taken over all the space he has left in his mind; even some of the area needed for other things has been taken hostage by her. The way her bright red hair lays over her shoulders like a silken burning flame is enough to make him question how he keeps himself in control around her. Everything about her compliments each other. Her pale skin is brought to life by her hair, which makes each tiny brown dot that spreads across her face even more noticeable. The brown of her eyes makes her light eyelashes become the tiniest stalks of grain, each one placed in her head with purpose.

Bashtian replays the mental image he has of her on loop because now it is his only comfort. Being back at the camp saddens him. Everyone there has someone, except for him. None of the single Demonians approach him anymore due to the amount of times he has rejected them, men and women alike.

His people have built homes where their tents once stood, and laughter fills the air in every moment. He cannot count all the new children anymore, but it does not stop the families from creating more. Bashtian dreams of having a little one to teach how to fly, walk, or anything. It was not until now that his dreams were filled with the pictures of a child. Before, his dreams would be faceless to him. It made them feel like if that dream did not come true, then he would be okay, but now the faceless child has features.

All of which have been plucked directly from Vanora, from the red hair to the shade of their skin. The only thing that makes him believe that he is father is the shape of the small wings on its back, and the darkness that lives under that pale, freckled skin.

Lowering his head towards his bent knees, Bashtian rubs his brow with his hand as his other arm drapes lazily over his knee. There is nothing he wants more than to get a night of rest without being pounded by dreams of someone who is supposed to be off limits and a made-up child that shares her face.

Etbris called for him the day after Vanora first followed him to the spot where he sits, and all he was told was to remember the Morals of Demonians. Specifically, one section in general: "I believe that each of you will make your own mark on this world, and it is only up to you if that is good or bad. I hope in a time of need, you never second-guess the faith and loyalty I have in you."

Bashtian has found himself repeating the words out loud and to himself as if they will give him an answer for his problems. He does not want to endanger anyone, especially Vanora. Lixtis is a dangerous being, and having her at his mercy is like waving a fresh, bloody carcass in front of a predator. If something were to happen between them, then he would have to tell Etbris. He would be the only one who would know what to do.

The still air around the creek begins to whistle as the sound of flapping follows soon after. Bashtian stands to his feet in an instant as his ears target the direction of the disturbance. The winged person is coming from directly to his right. None of his warriors knows where he is right now, and unless Vanora told their secret, then it should not be an Astrial either.

Slowly, his shoulders relax as he makes out the shape he has become accustomed to coming through the trees. It is Vanora. She should not be back this soon after leaving him, and with it being this bright in the day, anyone could have followed her or seen her from his camp. The last thing he wants is for her to be hunted by his warriors, but they are also content with their own lives.

Tucking a loose piece of his almost black hair behind his ear, Bashtian waits for the Angel to land. As her figure gets closer, he can make out the shape and color of her clothing. It is still the same set that she wore not even four hours ago. A pair of loose-fitting trousers the color of wet sand cover the expanse of her long legs. He wishes he knew if they were muscular or lean, if the same small freckles on her face spread across her pale skin.

The emerald-green blouse still drapes over her shoulders like the moss does the rocks just out of reach of the water; the laces that once made their way to the base of her throat now hang loose and leave a portion of her chest exposed to the rays of the sun. Her hair has been taken down from the plait she had it in after he and Vanora shared some cured meat earlier in their night. Everything about the woman slowly floating down to him is perfect, and the way the sun graces the white feathers on her back is something he will never grow tired of seeing. Bastian knows that because of them, wherever she goes, he can use those wings as a beacon and always find his way back to her.

On soundless feet, Vanora lands only a few feet in front of him. Bashtian does not say anything as he takes one more glance at everything that makes his enemy feel more like someone he can love.

"I need an answer." Her voice is quiet, but Bashtian catches every word she speaks and has ever spoken. They stay in a special place in his head to keep him company when he is away from her.

"Anything." He does not move an inch as Vanora's throat bobs and her tongue quickly wets her lips. Her eyes close as she takes in a steadying breath for just a moment.

"Kiss me?"

As the words register with Bashtian, he cannot help but to look at the spot her tongue had just touched. It feels like he is in one of his dreams because this is something that could only be possible there. That is until Vanora shifts her weight slightly as the silence between them grows heavy. Slowly, he takes a step towards her, his eyes searching hers to make sure he is not over-stepping any boundaries. A kiss. She wants a kiss from him. He does not have to think about the answer because he has already let this woman take over every part of him; she just does not know it.

Bashtian stops directly in front of Vanora, the tips of their leather boots touching enough for him to feel her toes move inside of hers. His arms are at his sides, just like hers. Their height is only two inches apart, which makes her look up at him. Those honey brown eyes drink in his facial features, and he lets her. The warmth of Vanora's gaze on his face is enough to make his body yearn to mold her body against his.

Vanoras's fingertips gently run across his as she asks again, "Kiss me?"

This time, Bashtian moves his hands to the side of her face. Looking into her eyes once more, his thumbs gently stroke the curves of her cheek bones, and ever so slowly he lowers his mouth to hers.

Their kiss begins with just a peck of his lips against hers before moving his face away. He wants to memorize the look of contentment on the face that haunts his dreams. Vanora has never looked as relaxed as she does now while her face is held in his hands.

The moment is over as soon as the hunger to taste every inch of her enters his body. Bashtian wants to set Vanora free. He wants to see her loosen the grip she has on herself and become the person she wants to be, the person he knows she is. Whatever has her trapped inside of herself, he wants to find it and tear its heart out, because no woman as perfect as this one should be troubled with as many demons as Vanora is.

As their lips touch this time, they both step further into each other's embrace. Vanora wraps her arms around his neck as he holds her head firmly in his grip. She fits to his body like a piece that has always been missing, and for once, he thinks Lixtis may have done one thing right with his existence.

With each passing second, their moves become more frantic as their desire begins to overflow from them both. Bashtian's breaths become quickened as Vanora tugs at the hair that rests at the base of his neck. His hands leave her face as his arms wrap around her back. With one hand resting at the base of her spine, the other just under her wings, Bashtian pulls away from their heated kiss.

"If we keep going, I do not think I will be able to stop." He takes a breath. "I dream about you every time I close my eyes. You even haunt me in the daylight, Vanora; if you want me to stop, then tell me now." His eyes look deep into hers to make sure he does not see any signs of a second guess.

"If I wanted you to stop, I would have told you already." Vanora runs a finger across his bottom lip. "This is not a dream, but I want you to show me what you do to me in them."

Bashtian drops his arms from her back as she takes a step away from him. He watches as she pulls the emerald-green top from her body, exposing her bare chest to him.

Bastian swallows the lump forming in his throat as he takes in the sight of her breasts. They are better than what his imagination came up with, but the light pink of her nipples is spot on. It only takes him a minute to decide; if this is what Vanora wants, then it is what she will get.

Today, in the forest of Baith, beside Cleansing Creek, and under the bright sun that makes Arugo his home, Bashtian will give into his desire for the Captain of the enemy army. He will allow himself this happiness once, and after, he will not indulge in the temptation of her anymore.

13

VANORA

After walking away from Elena by the fire this morning, Vanora did not expect to find herself in her current position. Finding Bashtian was supposed to bring her clarity as to why she has been consumed by the need to figure out who she is. He was going to answer the questions that she could not on her own, but instead she asked for a kiss. Seeing him made her forget everything she planned to say. It led to their lips touching and a flood of need spilling over what little restraint she had left.

A peck was not enough; even their passion-laced kiss was not enough to curve her crazing for the Demonian. Because of that, Vanora now stands naked in front of one of her biggest foes. Except right now, he looks more like a God as he slowly relieves his torso from the confines of the fabric of his top. His skin is kissed by the sun, and with each movement, the muscles that make up his frame show the true power that hides behind the layers he wears on the battlefield.

This time, she is the one to take a step back towards him. As she does, her hands immediately begin to trace each dip and curve of his abdomen. Different-sized scars scatter across his skin, and much like her own, Vanora thinks they show his power.

It takes power to be able to handle the way scars are obtained – some come from accident, some from purpose. They all have their own story, which gives the one that wears them power. Most of the ones she carries on her are from Lixtis, but she will not share that with anyone.

As her hands move up to his chest, Bashtian sucks in a breath. It draws Vanoras's attention away from the man who once had control of her every movement, and with the perfectly sculpted man in front of her, she will not allow herself to be anything but free.

"Can I touch you?" Bashtian's words are low, a light rumble carrying them out of his mouth and into her ears. It pulls her closer to him, pressing her body to hers as her mouth parts slightly. The feeling of her taut nipples against his warm skin is enough to make her lose her words.

Gently, he lowers his mouth so that it is centimeters from her own as he asks again, "Can I touch you?" The rumble that was there before seems to have faded just slightly; she pauses to consider if that is because he wonders if he scared her. Vanora ponders if he would think she is insane to find it a turn-on.

"Touch me." She moves her mouth just enough so each time her lips form a word, they dust across his. "Taste me." With a quick swipe of her tongue, Vanora licks Bashtian's lips. "Tease me."

With her permission, Bashtian wastes no time sending his hands to explore her bare skin as his lips paint kisses over every inch of her face. She cannot contain her moans as she savors the feeling of each purposeful touch. The sounds coming from her drive Bashtian mad because his movements become faster as he connects his lips with hers while picking her up by her backside.

The urge to grind herself against the spot where his trousers meet his hips is powerful enough to make her see stars, so Vanora does not stop herself. As her hips rock into Bashtian, he moves towards a tree that sits behind her back. Their lips do not get a break from each other until her back is set firmly against the tree, her wings pulled as flush to her as she can make them. They do not protest it, so she does not stop the man currently sinking to his knees as he holds her up by her thighs until they are draped over his shoulders. No words are said before Bashtian rubs two fingers down the lips between Vanora's legs. She sucks in a breath as he separates them and uses one of his fingers to find the entrance to her cunt.

Another moan leaves her as he slowly pushes the tip of his finger inside and places a kiss on her exposed clit. Vanora wants whatever he will give her, but if he moves any slower, she will start choking him with her thighs.

"Please," she says with pleading eyes as one of her hands moves to grip his hair.

Bashtian watches her as he gently glides his tongue over the spot he just kissed. Vanora's body grinds forward as her other hand grips the tree behind her head for added support.

"Beg me." Another pass of his tongue as his finger slides inside of her a touch more. "I want to hear you tell me what you want, Vanora. Tell me what you want me to do to you." His words send warmth over all her senses.

"I want you to taste every inch of me." Her breathing is faster than she wants it to be, but the way this man is looking at her makes her feel like she is the only thing to exist to him. "And then I want you to fuck me like I am yours."

Bashtian's free hand grips her side as he pulls his finger from its resting spot. "You are mine," he says, and the way his eyes darken tells Vanora that he is honest. She knows that it is too good to be true.

Without another word, he pushes his finger fully inside of her as he begins to satisfy her hunger for him by not letting a drop of her nectar fall to the ground. Her hips rock with each of his movements causing her nails to dig into the bark of the tree. With each stroke of his finger and lap of his tongue, Vanora edges closer to the verge of release.

"Stop." He immediately stops all his movements and looks up at her. It is the first time her words have ever held any power before. She almost forgets why she said it.

"I want you inside of me when I cum, not like this." Releasing the tree from her grip, Vanora tries to catch her breath as Bashtian takes her thighs from his shoulders and places her feet on the ground. He does not move away from her as he releases the two leather laces holding his trousers closed. Vanora watches with anticipation.

As he pushes his trousers to the ground and tosses them to the side, Vanora's mouth goes dry. Looking at the length of him makes her question where it is going to go. Bashtian pulls her to him by her hips as he plants a kiss on her lips.

"Are you sure?" His words are spoken low as his hands gently rub up and down her arms. The feeling of his calloused hands on her smooth skin sends chill bumps down her body.

"Yes." Vanora cannot lie to herself about not being nervous because she is. The only man she has ever slept with is also the same man who could kill her if he chose too. This time with Bashtian will be something she will cherish for the rest of her long life. It will even be the one thing she lets herself relive when all she wants to do is die.

Bashtian wraps one arm around her waist as the other grips her left ass cheek. Vanora wraps her legs around his midsection so that she is in the perfect position for him. As she relaxes in his hold, the tip of him lightly brushes against her lips, causing Bashtian to groan. Removing his grip from her ass, he centers himself with her entrance. Vanora gasps as he slowly lowers her body onto his length.

The sting feels amazing, and she wants more. Without giving any warning, Vanora digs her heels into Bashtian's lower back as she slides the rest of the way down his cock. Their heads both fall back at the same time, their hands holding onto each other until they regain control over their bodies. Once they can both steady their breathing, all of their control leaves.

Bashtian grips Vanora's ass in his hands as he begins to thrust himself deeper inside of her. Vanora is lost in the feeling of him not only being inside of her but of the memories of each gentle caress and every kind word he has spoken to her. She loses herself at the thought of building a family with someone who is completely off limits. They will share this night together, and then that must be it. Vanora will explain everything to Bashtian at the end of this, even though she never wants this to end.

As her moans grow louder, her body blooms with the warmth building from her core. She nears the point of no return, and Bashtian must know. His speed picks up as her legs tighten around his waist. The once perfect rhythm has become more sporadic. It is just what Vanora needs as she reaches her peak, and a slightly muffled scream escapes her lips. If it were not for Bashtian covering her mouth with his, then she would have scared away anything close to them.

It is not long after Vanora comes down from her high that she feels Bashtian slightly trembling underneath her. As he regains control over his body, they stay locked together, with Vanora's head resting on his shoulder, his forehead pressed into the skin of her neck. Her body never wants to separate from him, and that terrifies her.

Bashtian sinks to his knees while she is still wrapped in his embrace. Vanora does not stop him as the cool ground greets the bare skin of her ass. Taking his head from its resting place, she searches his eyes for any sign of regret, but what she finds is something like determination.

"What is it?" She must know what is going on with the warrior in front of her because the emotion he is showing is not one that she knows. Looking over his body to make sure he does not have any unknown wounds comes second nature to Vanora. Her time helping the menders at the camp shows through.

Bashtian rests his hand at the bottom of her jaw as his thumb lightly strokes her bottom lip. "I cannot let you go like I thought I could. From the moment I saw you standing tall in Battlements, I knew I would not be able to let you go. I told myself that I would when the time came, but I was a fool to think it would be that simple." His words are soft as they grace her skin with his heat.

"I did not come here for this." She waves a hand between their bare chests. "But when I saw you standing here, I could not contain myself. You have made me start to question everything."

Vanora takes his hand from her chin so she can interlock their fingers. "Nothing makes sense anymore, and I do not understand why I cannot get you out of my head." Her eyes burn as she swallows a lump in her throat.

"I can help you understand, Vanora. We can learn together. I do not know what our life will look like, but I will take anything I can get from you." Bashtian brings her hand to his mouth to place a small kiss on the back of it. "We are not what is right in this world, but I will fight every day to change that."

Vanora sighs as the reality of their situation sits heavy on her shoulders, but she cannot bring herself to care. She will accept any way of being with Bashtian, even if it means it will only be from their secret meetings in the night. "Whatever we must do is what will happen. We will figure it out together."

Bashtian's deep brown eyes catch the rays of sun peeking through the tree canopy as Vanora takes in every detail of them as he asks, "Together?"

With his question, she brings herself to her knees. "Together." She seals her promise with a kiss. Vanora is not sure how she has ended up in the arms of the Demonian Captain of Etbris's army, but it is too late to change it now.

The most concerning thing to her is that she does not want to change anything about this moment or the small ones that lead to it. She has grown more as a person being with Bashtian than she has under Lixtis's thumb. The feeling is worth more than anything another person can take away from her.

IV
BONDS MADE ANEW

1,507 A.B.

14

VANORA

Bashtian and Vanora sit in front of Etbris, even though all she wants to do is go back to their room. Ten years passed their secret meetings in the forest before Etbris confronted them. To her surprise, he was not angered by their relationship; instead, the God of Death seemed relieved. It also surprised Vanora that he was drastically different from his brother. Now, his stark white skin offset by his jet black features comfort her.

Sitting in this room with him like a child getting scolded on the other hand is anything but comforting. Bashtian was the one who called for this small gathering even after her pleas against it. She cannot blame him though because she is just as scared as he is. If they knew what to do, then they would not be in their current position.

Etbris is the only one Vanora trusts with the information they must share with him. They need all the advice and help they can get to know how to keep their predicament from overhearing ears and the rage of Lixtis.

The quietness of the room drives Vanora more insane with each passing second. Before she lets another one tick by, she looks at the God in his onyx eyes and says, "I am pregnant."

Bashtian snaps his head in her direction as his eyes widen, but she does not take hers from the God in front of her. She expects him to throw something at her or even kill her where she sits.

As the words leave the room, Etbris's smile grows wide as he looks into her eyes made of honey.

"That is wonderful! Congratulations to the both of you." His words make her shoulders relax as she reminds herself that Etbris is nothing like his elder brother. That is why Vanora spends most of her free time in the walls of his palace. She has found that she genuinely enjoys his company. He is also responsible for helping the couple have some time together because his shadows shroud them from his brother's light.

Vanora did not believe the stories Bashtian would tell her about his creator at first, but now she understands why all of his people are loyal to him without the use of scare tactics. Etbris is a kind soul who loves with everything that he has, unlike Lixtis, who would rather only have obedience.

"How are we going to keep this a secret once the babe starts to show?" Bashitan places a hand on her stomach without a second thought. It is something he has been doing since they found out four weeks ago.

"Do not worry about it. I will handle it; you two just need to worry about making sure that what you carry is safe and loved." Etbris smiles at them both as he tugs a strand of hair behind his ear.

Vanora trusts him with the secret of their unborn child, and that takes half of the concern off of her already crowded shoulders. All she wants is to have a family with the man she loves.

Right now, it does not seem so far out of reach.

EPILOGUE

THE DAY FINALLY CAME WHEN TWO SWORN ENEMIES, TURNED faithful partners, brought a new life into the world of Arugo. Their daughter entered into their arms when the sun hung in the sky the brightest; her cries made every individual around the birthing bed feel like the battle still being waged outside of the safety of Deaths Keep did not exist. For a moment, Bashtian, Vanora, Mariem, and Etbris all released relieved breaths for the new future they welcomed into their grief-stricken world. Little did they know that their happiness would soon come to an end before it even truly began.

The first cry from the child brought joy to the ones who could see her, but that single scream was full of power that none of them could imagine. It was something so powerful that when it made its way into the Nether to greet Light and Shadow, it ripped through the barrier, causing the two powers to separate from their constant flow side by side.

Shadow watched in awe as the new life burst into their home, while Light was left disgusted. The brightness did not like anything that took the attention of its partner away from the one perfect brother they created together, let alone something that would cause the space between itself and its love to be too wide to mend before their next meeting.

Shadow was content to let the destruction caused by the new life mend itself, even if it took more time than Light was willing to wait. The darkness enjoyed watching the young and old flow between the limits of life and death as Etbris helped guide each one. Light on the other hand, too consumed by rage to let the new life grow without punishment for the destruction it caused to the Nether.

It decided to send word to its favorite son, so that he could take care of the problem. Only Light did not know that the mother of that new life would choose to abandon her with a close friend where she would be shielded by the searching light of Lixtis by the son it hated.

It took Lixtis six hours after the birth of Vanora's daughter to find out what had been happening while he sat on this throne under the assumption that his Vanora was helping strengthen his army with the help of the Fae from Sytherac, Alister. When the God discovered the news of the betrayal, he sent his Light Hounds to his brother's home to send a message to the new mother, who lay in a bed nestled with her newborn.

The commotion of the Light Hounds and Shadow Hounds woke Vanora from her sleep just as Mariem came into the room to tell her of the danger that was sent to the palace door, along with the message that Lixtis knew about her daughter.

Bashtian stayed with the Shadow Hounds, keeping the others made of light at bay as Vanora consulted with Etbris and Mariem. The three of them planned to hide the child in shadows on Sytherac with someone Vanora trusted so that she would be out of harm's way. They had planned for Mariem to be the one to bring the babe, but that is not how it was in the end.

Vanora could not bring herself to let another woman take her daughter from her arms. She decided that the only way she would go through with the plan was if she was the one to drop her off. Etbris agreed hesitantly while Mariem refused to be a part of a plan that would cause Bashtian even more hurt than he would already find himself lost in, so she took the small hand into hers and said, "I will meet you again, Little Beast." It was all that she could say before tears streamed down her face.

That night, Vanora dressed in her white and gold armor and set her eyes to Sytherac. It took help from Etbris to harness enough of Lixtis's raw power from the Light Hounds to be able to open the path between the worlds, but it was done.

Before Bashtian made it back into their room, she was already flying over the different Kingdoms of Sytherac on the hunt for the one that was cloaked by nature. The babe slept like a rock in her arms as her wings carried her quietly to the front steps of the castle. All that Vanora could feel was shame and sadness; she had to leave a part of herself with the one person she trusts besides Bashtian, and that made her feel like a failure. If only the new mom knew what the future held for her daughter.

Without a word, Vanora gently laid the babe on the step closest to the grand stone doors of the castle. Gently, she placed a piece of parchment on the babes chest that read,

> *Take care of her.*
> *You owe us that much, Alister.*

With a gentle sweep of her finger, Vanora traced the surface of her daughter's forehead for the last time before she muttered the words, "Goodbye, Orien Ather." The sleeping babe resting on the steps of the stone castle, engulfed by the forest around it, only began to scream after her mother disappeared into the night.

Vanora's soul aches from the choices that have been made, but nothing is as ugly as the punishment waiting for her in the palace made of clouds and smoke. She will not return to the man who holds her soul in the palm of his hands because the man who made her will never stop searching for her. She will not allow her child's father to die in the hands of someone as cruel as Lixtis. Even if it means she must endure a lifetime of punishment.

Tears streamed down her face as she spoke to the darkness of the clouds above her, "I am ready." and right before her eyes, the familiar shadows that once greeted her in the hallways of Deaths Keep faded away. She was left exposed to the eyes that were searching for her, and it did not take long for them to find her and drag her back to their home.

The new life she had made on the outside of Souls Haven lay in a tattered heap.

The tent that once stood tall, now is nothing more than ragged cloth left to sink into the damp soil of Lorenon.

The man she loves is left alone, confused about where not only his mate went but his newly born child. It did not take long for the anguished screams of Bashtian to reach her as her body glided into the arms of a stone-faced man who had always used her as nothing more than property. Gone was the sense of true love, pleasure, and acceptance. In its place, the familiar claws of pain, sorrow, and longing strangled the heart in her chest.

This is the mess she caused by chasing a dream that should have stayed in the faraway spaces in her mind. Now, her suffering will become fuel for a God hell bent on revenge. The babe she birthed, his newest obsession until he creates one of his own with a woman he has been waiting for her for hundreds of years. A woman who can see the suggestions of the future before it happens, but nothing will compare to the hurt that resides inside the Astrial Angel who is trapped in the sinister web of her creator.

Vanora will never forgive herself for the harm she has caused to so many lives, but nothing will overpower the hatred she has for herself.

Moral of Demonians

The Law of Demonians is described as a set of morals that each Demonian is to hear by but is not forced to follow.
Etbris hopes his Demonians will live out long lives that are filled with many triumphs. He created this set of morals so that everyone can look back and use his words as a tool of guidance if they should ever find themselves to need them. These are spoken directly from the God of Death, Etbris, and should never be taken lightly.

....

To my children, I hope you can use my words to help you find your way if you should ever need them.

I created each of you to differ from the other. No two of you are the same, and that is something you should be proud of. You are meant to be yourself and not like anyone else. I made you who you are meant to be.

Nothing you do will make me love you less. I do not say those words lightly, so know that I mean it. Disappointment is far different from unloving. If your heart is telling you that you need to complete a goal that is against what I see fit, then search in your heart to see if you are making the right choice. I can be a guiding voice, but I cannot make tough decisions for you.

Every living creature needs to be treated as you would want to be treated. This world is like many others that were made, so know that you were not made first. You do not get more say than any animal or plant that lives beside you just because you may feel more powerful. Arugo was not meant to cater to you, and you are not the most important thing that lives here. It takes the lives of thousands to make our world what it is – a home.

Moral of Demonians

Just because something is different does not mean that it is bad. I want you to understand that. Each of you has distinctive characteristics that make you stand out from the next, and that is how it is supposed to be. Nothing is wrong with looking like yourself. Do not change yourself to seek approval or acceptance from others.

Think about your words before you speak them. Words are the number one weapon in any situation, not just conflict. The things you say to someone cannot be taken back, and the wounds that can be left behind do not heal like the physical.

Respect yourself and everyone around you. Everyone you meet should be shown some type of respect, even if they are your enemy. Not everyone is bad. Sometimes, a poisoned voice makes them feel that way. Be the one that can share a good death even with a serpent in disguise, but never let it close enough to bite.

If you should have children, teach them the fundamentals of what it takes to be a brave warrior: honesty, integrity, self-worth, and understanding that a war does not mean the end.

I believe that each of you will make your own mark on this world, and it is only up to you if that is good or bad. I hope in a time of need you never second-guess the faith and loyalty I have in you. Creating you has been my number one honor, and if I should be taken from this plane of existence before my natural time, I hope I have not failed any of you.

From now until thereafter, I will always love you.

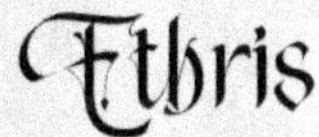

Law of Astrial Angels

The Law of Astrial Angels is set in place to ensure that every Angel is held to the same standard as the first that was created. The master, Lixtis, found these laws himself, and therefore they are held to the highest authority. If at any time an Angel is caught not obeying the Law of Astrial Angels, their wings will be ripped from their sockets, and their body will be disposed of accordingly.

· All Angels must show their thankfulness to their master for the life they are given.

· No Angel is to breed outside of their own race. To do so means termination of the female and abomination to which she carries.

· No Angel should allow another race to speak ill will on their master's name. He is to only be held in the highest of manners.

· Every Angel must fight in The Eternal War as well as produce heirs to help repopulate the army.

· No one, male or female, is allowed to say no to their master's wishes. No matter what they may be.

· No Angel is to carry the weight of a child made by the master himself. If a female is found to be with a child after laying with the master, it is to be terminated, and the Angel will be made sterile so that it does not happen again.

· Any Angel that is caught sharing any information about their master with any other race will be put to death, and their name will be made a laughingstock to the rest of the Angels.

Law of Astrial Angels

· No information about Souls Heaven, the home of Lixtis, will be shared or talked about in any manner. His home should always remain a mystery to anyone who has not been granted permission to step foot past the thicket of clouds and fog. That includes Angels.

· Angels should never say any words of praise for the lower God and brother of the master. If caught doing so, then their life will be taken.

These Laws are to always be followed and frequently watched, as the master can add any new ones he sees fit. It is the Angels job to study these Laws as they are written and force them to memory. Any Angel can be called upon at any time to recite these Laws and to not know them by heart and soul means you are no longer loyal to the master and God of Souls, Lixtis.

Timeline

0 A.B.

Lixtis and Etbris are born from Light and Shadow.

1 A.B.

Light and Shadow make a home for their sons.

1 A.B. - 448 A.B.

The brothers claim their land and create their palaces. All while understanding their powers.

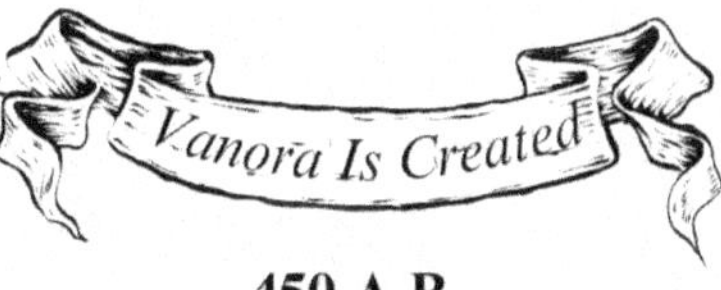

450 A.B.

Lixtis is lonely and decides he wants to test his abilities, he creates Vanora.

455 A.B.

Etbris creates his first creation, Shadow Hounds.

456 A.B.

Lixtis creates Light Hounds out of jealousy.

460 A.B. - 470 A.B.

Etbris spends his time creating many different species.

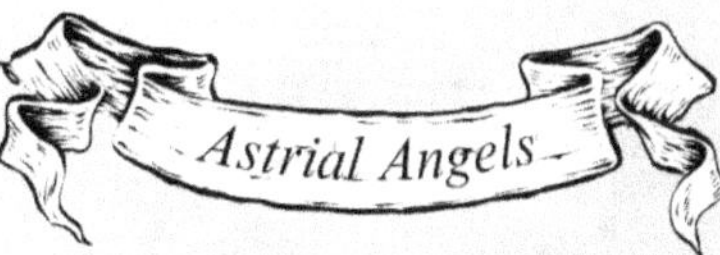

460 A.B. - Until Present

Lixtis decides to create more bodies to surround himself with. He creates the Astrial Angels.

500 A.B.

Etbris creates Sytherac, a world specifically for his creations.

690 A.B.

Lixtis sends the Astrial and Light Hounds to slaughter all of Etbris's creations on Sytherac.

Timeline

Bashtian Is Created
690 A.B.
Etbris creates the first Demonian out of the anger for his brother's actions.

Banished Demonian
697 A.B.
Morzon is the first Demonian banished to Sytherac.

Hartland Falls
699 A.B.
Hartland is banished from Arugo. Establishes Thundaria.

Sandur Falls
706 A.B.
Sandur is banished from Arugo. Establishes Desitae.

War Begins
800 A.B.
The Eternal War begins.

Building Armies
690 A.B.
Lixtis and Etbris start building their armies and creating battle plans.

Altairien Falls
699 A.B.
Altairien is banished from Arugo. Establishes Univier.

Kav Falls
703 A.B.
Kav is banished from Arugo. Establishes Runearid.

Nepatae Falls
707 A.B.
Nepatae is banished from Arugo. Establishes Octovah.

Fredrick
878 A.B.
Fredrick is born to his parents in Thundaria.

Timeline

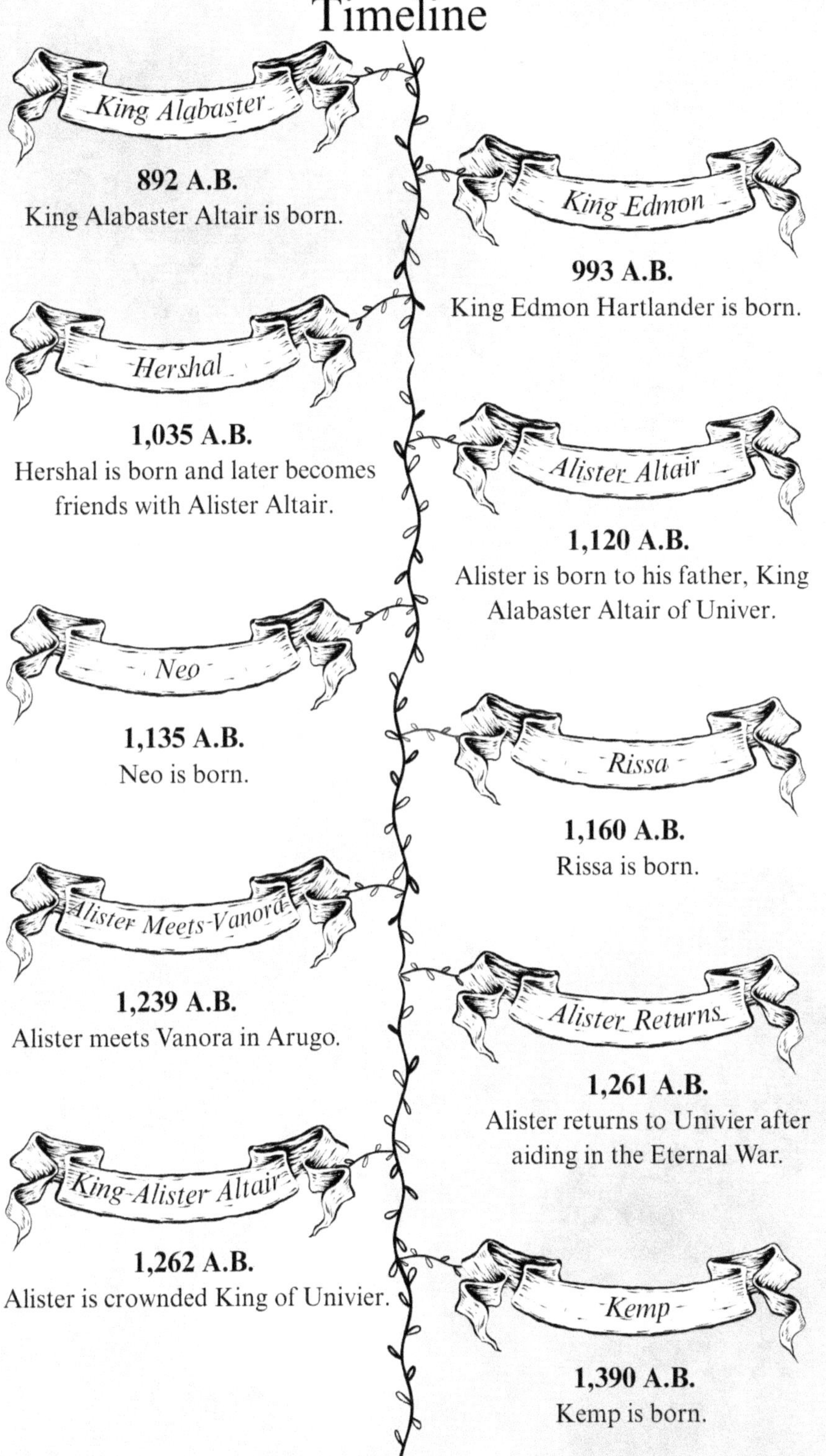

King Alabaster
892 A.B.
King Alabaster Altair is born.

Hershal
1,035 A.B.
Hershal is born and later becomes friends with Alister Altair.

Neo
1,135 A.B.
Neo is born.

Alister Meets Vanora
1,239 A.B.
Alister meets Vanora in Arugo.

King Alister Altair
1,262 A.B.
Alister is crownded King of Univier.

King Edmon
993 A.B.
King Edmon Hartlander is born.

Alister Altair
1,120 A.B.
Alister is born to his father, King Alabaster Altair of Univer.

Rissa
1,160 A.B.
Rissa is born.

Alister Returns
1,261 A.B.
Alister returns to Univier after aiding in the Eternal War.

Kemp
1,390 A.B.
Kemp is born.

Timeline

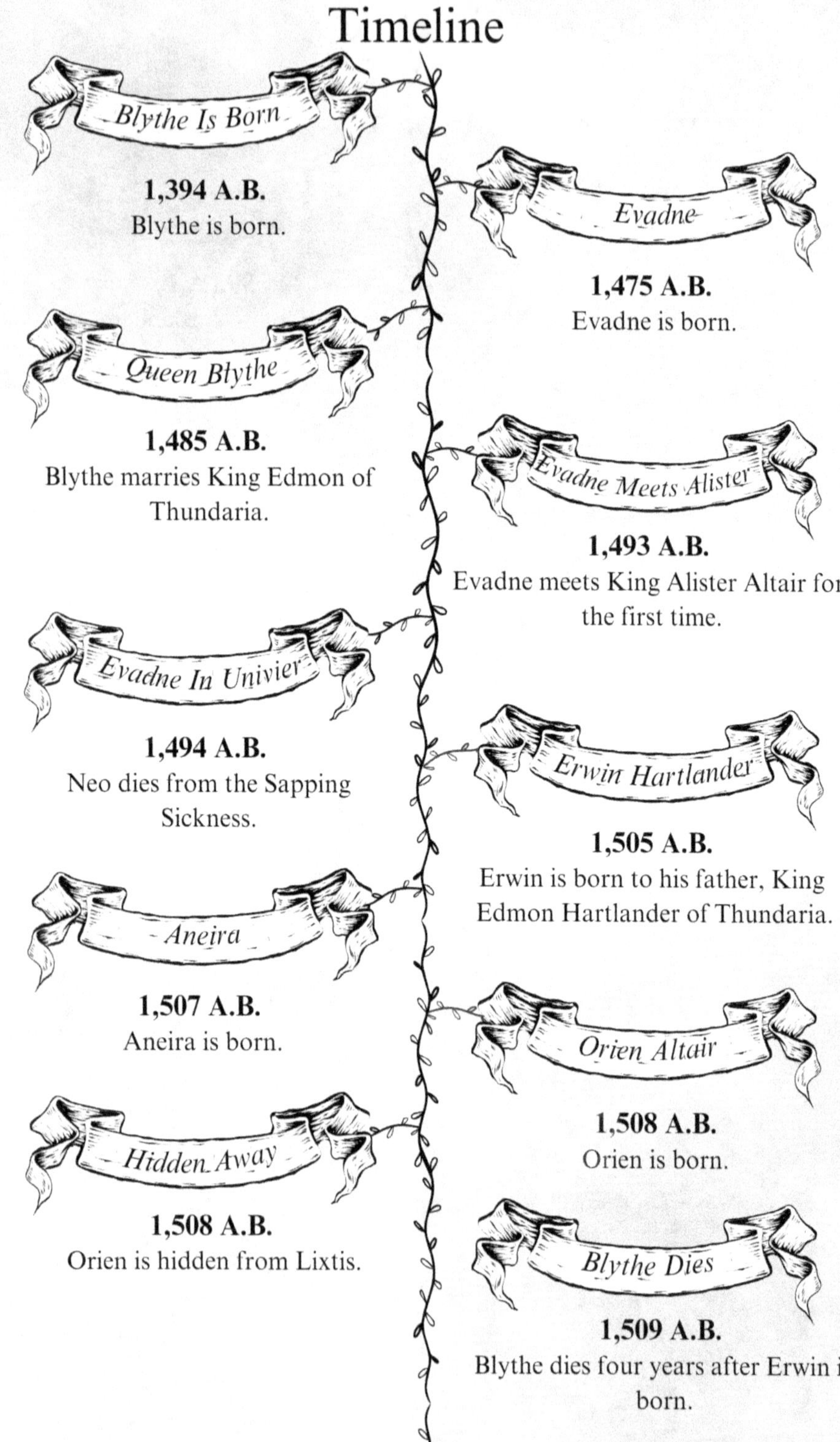

Blythe Is Born
1,394 A.B.
Blythe is born.

Evadne
1,475 A.B.
Evadne is born.

Queen Blythe
1,485 A.B.
Blythe marries King Edmon of Thundaria.

Evadne Meets Alister
1,493 A.B.
Evadne meets King Alister Altair for the first time.

Evadne In Univier
1,494 A.B.
Neo dies from the Sapping Sickness.

Erwin Hartlander
1,505 A.B.
Erwin is born to his father, King Edmon Hartlander of Thundaria.

Aneira
1,507 A.B.
Aneira is born.

Orien Altair
1,508 A.B.
Orien is born.

Hidden Away
1,508 A.B.
Orien is hidden from Lixtis.

Blythe Dies
1,509 A.B.
Blythe dies four years after Erwin is born.

Timeline

Elisiah Reindale

1,511 A.B.
Elisiah is born.

The Muzzle

1,513 A.B.
Orien receives The muzzle.

Neo Dies

1,517 A.B.
Neo dies from the Sapping
Sickness.

King Edmon Dies

1,534 A.B.
King Edmon dies from the
Sapping Sickness.

The First Scar

1,513 A.B.
Orien receives the first scar on
her hand.

Sapping Sickness

1,514 A.B.
The Sapping Sickness spreads
across Thundaria.

Sterilization

1,518 A.B.
Orien is sterilized.

Present Day

1,535 A.B.
Present day for the current event
in Ruptured Light.

ACKNOWLEDGMENTS

Tainted Bonds would not have become what it is without the support of a few great people. I want to take the time to thank those who have never given up on me and have seen my worth even when I did not see it myself.

My wonderful husband, what would I do without you? You do your best to keep me sane every day as well as encourage me to reach beyond the stars. You have always seen me for who I am and taught me that having a backbone is worth more than seeking approval. I am going to keep it short this time around, but just know that a lot of Bashtian is based off of you. Two tough cookies who would do anything for the ones they love.

The Byles Family I am eternally grateful that we have crossed paths. Getting the chance to know all of you has only brought my small family nothing but smiles. Thank you for loving not only my babies but also my husband. I can not put into words how much it means to me that you all take the time to uplift my husband, showing him that all of his hard work is worth something. Thank you for listening to every story I tell about my dreams of becoming a bestselling author one day. I hope you all know how much your family means to ours, but most importantly, how much we love you all! Keep being the wonderful people you are because you have changed us for the better one kind word at a time.

Beth Hudson I just love you! I truly do not know what I would have done if I did not find you. Ruptured Light was in dire need of saving, and your words inspired me to not only continue writing but also better my craft. I know Tainted Bonds has taken a while for me to write, but I hope you can see my growth with each word. I know you are an editor, but for me you are so much more! I could not have asked for a better editor, teacher, or friend. I hope you never get tired of me.

Amanda Johnson I just love you too! I am always excited to tell anyone that will listen that I got to meet you and your husband. Not only have you saved me from the confusion that comes along with publishing, but you have also taught me how to tackle it on my own. Just know that I have taken notes and have implemented using a schedule for all of my planning. I can not believe how extraordinary you are at your job! You always impress me with the amount of stuff you tackle daily. I guess that is why you are amazing at schedule keeping! Thank you for leading me to Beth and lifting me up as a new author. I hope you don't get tired of me either because I am here to stay.

My readers I want to take a moment to say how grateful I am that you have taken the time to read my words. I hope that it was worth it for you, and that you liked it enough to keep on reading. I strive to become better every day so that you have the best experience while reading my books. My socials are always open for any comments you may need to make! I hope your days are always full of warmth and laughter.

From now until thereafter, I will always love you.

K.R. Richard

ABOUT THE AUTHOR

K.R. Richard writes epic fantasy novels with massive worlds and intricate characters.

Writing has always been her safe space, and words began to make their way from her imagination to the page at the early age of 9. She didn't know how to cope with feelings that seemed insurmountable, so she wrote about them instead.

After her sister passed, she picked up books, but when she couldn't find the one that said what she wanted to read, she decided to write her own.

She lives in the south with her high-school sweetheart, where they raise three kiddos and remember the one with angel wings.

facebook.com/k.r.richard.author

instagram.com/k.r.richard_author

tiktok.com/@krrichard_fantasyauthor